THE JOY OF FLIGHT - COLOR EDITION
SLIPPING THE SURLY BONDS

GARY R. WILSON

COPYRIGHT

Copyright © 2024 by Gary R. Wilson

All rights reserved.

ISBN: 9798323217533

Available on Amazon

First printing 2024

Printed in the United States of America

"Unless otherwise indicated, all Scripture quotations are from The ESV®Bible (The Holy Bible, English Standard Version®, copyright © 2001 by Crossway, a publishing ministry of Good News Publishers. Used by permission. All rights reserved."

Any internet addresses (websites, blogs, etc.) or telephone numbers in this book are offered as a resource only. They are not intended in any way to be or imply an endorsement by Amazon, nor does Amazon vouch for the contents of these sites and numbers for the life of this book. All quoted material was taken from the internet unless otherwise stated.

Italics or parentheses in any scripture reference are the author's emphasis.

Cover design by author

Cover photo courtesy of Richard Coke Marshall, 74th Recon Airplane Company, Vietnam, 1970

Photos not generated by the author are in the public domain or are used by permission.

Some photos were edited to improve the quality of an illustration.

For my Children

CONTENTS

Also by Gary R. Wilson	6
Introduction	7
Preface	11
1. You're in the Army Now	15
2. Officer Candidate School	18
3. 1967 - Summer of Love	23
4. Army Flight Training	27
5. Welcome to Vietnam	38
6. On the Job Training	43
7. Low and Slow	46
8. Taking Fire	49
9. Tây Ninh	53
10. Xuân Lộc	56
11. A Wing and a Prayer	59
12. Oops and Congratulations	61
13. Hàm Tân	64
14. R&R	68
15. Medals and Doubts	72
16. Night Flying	75
17. Going Home	79
18. Alaska	81
19. Kenai	89
20. Kodiak Island	92
21. Caribou Hunting	96
22. Fort Yukon	101
23. Mickey Mouse	105
24. Nome	107
25. Saint Lawrence Island	114
26. Search & Rescue	117
27. The Wood River	121
28. Valdez	126

29. Dall Sheep	130
30. Mt. Pavlof Volcano	135
31. Fort Greely	138
32. Kotzebue	141
33. Flying into Midnight	143
34. Barrow	151
35. Leaving Alaska	155
Afterword	161
About the Author	171

ALSO BY GARY R. WILSON

MEMORIES: RECIPES FROM CALLOWAY CORNERS, LOUISIANA

PERSPECTIVE: THE BIBLE and other INCONVENIENT TRUTHS

THERE'S SOMETHING ABOUT A WOMAN: GOD'S GIFT TO MANKIND

WHERE THE EYES LEAD: A BIKER'S CODE TO UNLOCKING THE BIBLE

IT'S ALL ABOUT JESUS: APOLOGETICS MADE SIMPLE

LEST ANY SHOULD BOAST: IT'S A GIFT, NOT A PROFESSION

A BOX OF CHOCOLATES: HUMBLE IS AS HUMBLE DOES

HAVE YOU NOT READ?: REVELATION 1:1-3

ROMANS: A CRITICAL EXPOSÉ

EPHESIANS: A CRITICAL EXPOSÉ

ECSTASY LOST: ONE FLESH FOREVER?

A TIGER TALE or A TALE ABOUT A TIGER'S TAIL

EXPRESSIONS OF MYSELF: POEMS, SHORT STORIES & OTHER RAMBLINGS

INTRODUCTION

"But they who wait for the Lord shall renew their strength; they shall mount up with wings like eagles." **(Isaiah 40:31)**

High Flight — BY JOHN GILLESPIE MAGEE JR.
    Oh! I have slipped the surly bonds of Earth
    And danced the skies on laughter-silvered wings;
    Sunward I've climbed, and joined the tumbling mirth
    of sun-split clouds,—and done a hundred things
    You have not dreamed of—wheeled and soared and swung
    High in the sunlit silence. Hov'ring there,
    I've chased the shouting wind along and flung
    My eager craft through footless halls of air ....
    Up, up the long, delirious, burning blue
    I've topped the wind-swept heights with easy grace
    Where never lark nor ever eagle flew—
    And, while with silent lifting mind I've trod
    The high untrespassed sanctity of space,
    Put out my hand, and touched the face of God.

INTRODUCTION

"**High Flight** *is a 1941 sonnet written by war poet John Gillespie Magee Jr. and inspired by his experiences as a fighter pilot of the Royal Canadian Air Force in World War II. Magee began writing the poem on 18 August while stationed at No. 53 OTU outside London and mailed a completed manuscript to his family on 3 September, three months before he died in a training accident. Originally published in the Pittsburgh Post-Gazette, it was widely distributed when Magee became one of the first post-Pearl Harbor American casualties of the war on 11 December. It was later exhibited at the American Library of Congress in 1942. Owing to its [euphoric] and ethereal portrayal of aviation and its allegorical interpretation of death and transcendence, the poem has been featured prominently in aviation memorials worldwide, including that of the Space Shuttle Challenger disaster.*" — **Wikipedia**

As the years pass, I find myself increasingly pondering my life choices. I've been fortunate to experience many exciting adventures and witness many of the beauties of our world, yet I have also had moments of regret.

Although he died of cancer when I was ten, *I know my daddy loved me unconditionally, and he taught me to love God and others by living it in his daily walk. He was my hero.*

My greatest regret is that, due to divorce, I wasn't there for my children when they needed me. I love my children, and they love me, but I will never hear them say....... *"My Daddy loved me unconditionally. He taught me to love God and others by living it in his daily walk. He was my hero."*

So, this book is for my children. I find myself trying to end my life's journey by leaving some positive legacy to them in my books. They all include affirmation and documentation that God's love is steadfast and unchanging, and through a belief in His Son, Jesus, we can live with Him someday. Though we may grow distant from Him or fickle in our attitude toward Him, His love for us never changes.

INTRODUCTION

But this is a book about flight, so let's talk about flying! One of the biggest pleasures of flying airplanes is the freedom it provides. It is exciting not only to go virtually anywhere at any time but also to explore things you have never seen before from a bird's-eye view. It's flying "outside" the cockpit.

> *"In the billions of hours that men have been aloft, not one has left a mark in the sky. Into the smooth sky, we pull a tiny wake of rippled air. When our airplane is gone, the sky smooths, carefully covering every sign of our passing, and becomes the quiet wilderness that it has always been."* —
> **Richard Bach**

Pilots willing to push beyond the narrow realm of modern navigation aids reap the rewards of seeing the country's magnificence from the intimate aerial perspective that only VFR (Visual Flight Rules) flying provides.

The sights and sensations of flying VFR allow us to get "outside" the cockpit and really see what's out there. Except under IFR (Instrument Flight Rules) conditions, enabling artificial intelligence to do our work for us puts us in a box and removes all sense of daring, adventure, and the "freedom" of flight. Getting "outside" the cockpit also allows us to practice and hone our skills as pilots and develop situational awareness.

Situational awareness or SA means having a mental picture of the existing interrelationship of location, flight conditions, configuration, and energy state of your aircraft as well as any other factors that could be about to affect its safety, such as proximate terrain, obstructions, airspace clearance, and weather systems.

Part of the joy of flight is discovering some intriguing new spot on the ground. When you do, you can land and explore further, as you will find by continuing to read. However, flying without artificial intelligence or air traffic control constraints is the only way to truly explore from the air.

INTRODUCTION

As John Gillespie Magee expressed in his sonnet, I, too, have *"topped the wind-swept heights....... and touched the face of God."* As a bird's natural instinct, not its wings, determines how well it can fly, I will fly like the eagle that flies as if it never remembered it was once an egg! Come along with me and experience the excitement, adventure, and "The Joy of Flight."

"When once you have tasted flight, you will forever walk the earth with your eyes turned skyward. For there you have been, and there you will always long to return" — **Leonardo da Vinci**

How did he know that?

PREFACE

The joy of flight feels too God-like to be attained by man....... until you have an engine failure.

Flight has progressed from barely flyable projectiles to things that hover, climb straight up, or zip through the air at many hundreds of miles an hour, but that is not what this book is about. It is about the joy and magical experience of flight.

When you push the throttle in or roll the power on and initiate that first gentle shudder of anticipation, there is the raw feel of something magical in that moment. Objects begin to blur, and the landscape speeds past. Then, with a gentle tug on the yoke or a lift of the collective and a forward movement of the cyclic, a moment of pure joy is realized. The aircraft lifts off, and the earth recedes quickly below you. Buildings and trees fall away as you climb into the sky.

It doesn't matter if the sky is blue, gray, or black; the aerodynamic forces are in control, yielding only to thrust and lift to counter drag and weight. The sound of the engine becomes a constant and welcome music. The aircraft responds majestically to the pilot's control. There is a certain magic in the flight of any aircraft. It is felt, imagined, and experienced at a deeper level than any other; then, it is captured in the treasury of the pilot's memory bank.

A pilot's experiences transcend the boundaries of ordinary existence. As they navigate the vast expanse of the sky, pilots encounter challenges, triumphs, and moments of profound reflection. Beyond the technical skills and aeronautical knowledge of flight, the cockpit becomes a school where valuable lessons about themselves are learned as they fly their aircraft as passionately and smoothly as an artist carefully brushes his paintbrush along his painting.

In four years of Army aviation, I flew 2,155 hours and saw and experienced many extraordinary things that mere land-bound mortals have never witnessed. I have flown in the tropics and the extreme cold of arctic winters in single-engine and multi-engine airplanes—airplanes with tricycle gear, airplanes with tail wheels, and helicopters.

Flying a helicopter is one of the most beautiful, inspiring, and glorious things a man can experience. It is like an art form. Helicopter pilots fly their aircraft like a hummingbird controls the air that surrounds it. They move along the landscape, following the contours like eagles gliding on air currents, rising effortlessly to clear trees, banking, climbing, and descending like swifts after their prey. Their hands and feet on the controls move with the delicacy of coordination of Chet Atkins' or Earl Klugh's sure and seemingly effortless hands on their guitars, moving as one with their rotary steeds.

In Vietnam, I flew above triple-canopied jungles so close I could almost reach down and touch them. Flight was strictly VFR, whether at night or during the day. You had to "see" where you were going.

In Alaska, I flew through valleys, along rivers, and above and around snow-covered mountains. I flew above, around, and through snowy clouds and their valleys. The vistas and views from above are

PREFACE

incomparable to views that, on the earth's surface, are limited to lateral ones and those interrupted by man-made obstacles.

I have ventured into the darkness of clouds, rain, snow, and icing conditions with only instrument guidance, listening to the reassuring hum of twin turboprop engines. I have climbed above those clouds and seen the rising sun casting its glow across this soft, cottony cloudscape where a few mountain peaks dared protest and break above the clouds. There is joy, pure and simple, in those moments. Nothing matches, compares, or even comes close to equaling it.

From the vantage point of flight, the world appears different, calm, quiet, and almost magical. Human occupation gives way to the natural majesty of mountains, rivers, forests, and lakes. Looking below at this wonder of nature, crafted over thousands of years, and marveling at the ability to see it in all its natural beauty is truly an awesome view to behold.

Nature paints breathtaking pictures.

The winds aloft can sometimes be brutal, bucking against the aircraft at 30 to 70 miles an hour, slowing you down or perhaps at times, helping you zip along feeling like Top Gun's Maverick ("I feel the need for speed").

But, mostly, it's relatively calm and quiet up there. There's only the occasional chatter between Air Traffic Control and other pilots. There is politeness even among the harried controllers handling simultaneous arrivals and departures at airports. Everyone seems to love what they do in aviation, which is a great blessing while flying.

As the aerodynamic forces of thrust overcome drag and weight to lift the aircraft off the earth's surface, the same forces under the pilot's control bring it down. Pulling back on the throttle or rolling off the power, adding drag in the form of landing gear or flaps, or lowering the collective and gently pulling back on the cyclic helps gravity bring the aircraft back to its bond with the earth.

The pilot lines his aircraft up with the distant runway and, drawing on hours of experience, manages its controls and power to gently bring it safely down onto the runway. The flight ends with the chirp of tires or the transition from flight to hover. Once the aircraft is shut down and secured, the pilot's work is done.

∼

But the joy of flight remains in his memory.

CHAPTER 1
YOU'RE IN THE ARMY NOW

It was a beautiful fall day in October 1965. I was sitting in a first-year math class at Hardin-Simmons University in Abilene, Texas, staring out the window. I was imagining the "freedom" of being on a naval ship out on the open sea.

As soon as class was over, I headed for the courthouse where the recruiting offices were located. When I found the naval recruiting office, I went inside and told the recruiter I wanted to join the Navy. He asked me if I had an assignment preference, and I replied, *"Nuclear submarines."* Nuclear submarines?! Not an hour ago, I had been daydreaming of being out on the "open" ocean!

The recruiter said I had to take a one-hundred-question exam to determine whether I qualified for placement on nuclear submarines. I maxed the exam. I was really excited and couldn't wait to get back on campus to tell my "Army" ROTC cadet company commander what I had done. Did I mention that I was a very gung-ho Army ROTC cadet?

When I arrived at his room, he was busy studying for an exam. I said, *"You'll never guess what I just did." "Knowing you, it could be anything, but I haven't got time for this right now,"* he responded. I told him that I had just joined the Navy, and he said, *"You have not joined the Navy. Now, go away and leave me alone."* I told him that I really had joined the Navy, and he repeated his first reply to me. Once again, I told him that I had really joined the Navy.

He laid down his pencil, leaned back in his chair, and looked at me. Until now, he had not bothered to look up from what he was studying. He said, *"I thought you wanted to be an officer and go to flight school."* I replied that I did. He smiled and said, *"Only in the Army can you be an officer and go to flight school without at least a bachelor's degree."*

I headed back to the courthouse, found the Army recruiter's office, which was across the hall from the Navy recruiting office, and told the Army recruiter I wanted to join the Army, but I had just joined the Navy. He said, *"No problem."* He then went across the hall to get my papers and signed me up.

Drill Sergeants

I ENLISTED FOR AIRBORNE INFANTRY. After completing basic training at Fort Polk, Louisiana, I was sent to military police training at Fort Gordon, Georgia! I had been "guaranteed" airborne infantry, but I was going to MP school instead.

. . .

My Basic Training Platoon at Graduation

I APPLIED for Officer Candidate School while there and listed my choice as infantry. I was later interviewed by a panel of three MP officers, two captains, and a major. Wrapping up the interview, the major said, *"I see you have listed infantry as your only interest for OCS. What's wrong with the MPs?"* I replied, *"Nothing, sir, but I want to be in the infantry."* He said, *"Fair enough,"* and signed my application.

WHILE IN OCS, I applied for flight school. For the rest of the story, continue reading.

CHAPTER 2
OFFICER CANDIDATE SCHOOL

Officer Candidate School was established in 1941 when the Secretary of the War Department — the original name of the Defense Department — and the Army Chief of Staff saw a need for a faster program to commission officers.

That spring, the Selective Service Program had brought close to a million new soldiers to the Army, significantly increasing the need for officers. September 2017 marked the 75th anniversary of the graduation of the first OCS class.

From 1964 to 1973, the Infantry Officer Candidate School (OCS) at Fort Benning, Georgia, produced approximately 29,000 Second Lieutenants. Most served one or more tours of duty in Vietnam. There were thousands of battlefield heroes and many thousands of casualties among the graduates of the various OCS programs during Vietnam. During the Vietnam War, nineteen Fort Benning OCS program graduates were awarded the Medal of Honor.

The 104 men selected by the U.S. Army for class 1-67 of the 63rd Infantry Officer Candidate Company, of which I was one, began their rigorous training in July 1966. These candidates came to Fort Benning with widely diverse ranks and levels of experience. Some were E-3s just months out of basic training, like me. Others were of higher NCO or warrant officer ranks with years of experience. All of us received at least E-5 pay until graduation.

I'm at the left end of the row next to the Candidate Battalion Commander.

WE WERE GROUPED ALPHABETICALLY into five platoons, regardless of age, rank, and military experience. Those of us who made it were drawn together by our shared desire to succeed and excel. Our broad range of experience and determination bound us into a strong company of officer candidates.

"This is going to be a long haul."

We enjoyed things such as dropping for pushups for looking at a Tac Officer wrong or other inane reasons, middle-of-the-night wake-ups with Tac Officers screaming at us to fall out in full field gear, and going on marches through Georgia's woods and fields.

After six months of intense training in Georgia's sun, heat, cold, and rain, 102 of us were commissioned as second Lieutenants in January 1967. Most of us were second lieutenants of Infantry; some went on to Special Forces, Army Intelligence, Engineer, Quartermaster Corps, Signal Corps, and Aviation.

MANY OF THOSE newly commissioned officers saw service in Vietnam within one year of graduation. Many died in service to their country in that war.

Among class 1-67 of the 63rd OCS graduates were officers who were highly decorated for valor and heroism in Vietnam. They earned such awards as the Distinguished Service Cross, the Silver Star, the Distinguished Flying Cross, the Bronze Star for Valor in Combat, the Vietnamese Cross of Gallantry, and Purple Hearts. Many received Combat Infantry Badges, Air Medals, and other awards and badges of distinction.

The highest award I earned in Vietnam was the Distinguished Flying Cross. Others were the Bronze Star, the Air Medal with 25 Oak Leaf Clusters, the Vietnamese Cross of Gallantry with Bronze Star, and numerous lesser medals.

WHILE A SENIOR CANDIDATE, I traded my 1966 Chevy for a new 1967 Austin Healey 3000 Mk3 British Sports car.

Upon graduation, I drove to Fort Knox, Kentucky, for three months of training in Organizational Maintenance for Officers.

There, I learned Field-Level Maintenance for all reportable and non-reportable equipment, including vehicles from the M-151 Jeep to the M-60 Main Battle Tank and weapons from the model 1911 .45 caliber pistol to the 8-inch self-propelled howitzer.

Other services included technical inspections, estimating costs for damage and repairs, and maintenance expenditure limit tracking.

My next assignment was as a training officer in a basic training unit at Fort Ord, California. I was headed for the "Summer of Love."

CHAPTER 3
1967 - SUMMER OF LOVE

*The **Summer of Love** was a major social phenomenon that occurred in San Francisco and Monterey, California, during the summer of 1967. An episode of the PBS documentary series American Experience referred to it as "the largest migration of young people in the history of America."*

Held at the Monterey County Fairgrounds from June 16-18, 1967, the Monterey Pop Festival attracted around 200,000 people. It was the first major rock festival in America. The event was organized by Lou Adler, John Phillips of The Mamas & The Papas, and Derek Taylor, the former Beatles publicist. Their ambition was to create a multi-cultural, multi-national, and multi-genre event. It was indeed a "first," and it can be considered the premier event of the "Summer of Love," where everything seemed to work and about which little bad has ever been written.

Although the Fantasy Faire at Mount Tamalpais in California was first, the Monterey Pop Festival is the one everyone remembers, with a line-up that read like a who's who in pop music. Otis Redding got his first exposure to a rock audience, and others on the bill included The Mamas & The Papas, Jimi Hendrix, The Who, Janis Joplin, and Ravi Shankar. D. A. Pennebaker captured it all on film, greatly enhancing its reputation (and myth). This was the very epicenter of the "Summer of Love."

The Complete Lineup

The Who, Steve Miller Band, The Animals, Simon & Garfunkel, Buffalo Springfield, Grateful Dead, Booker T & The MG's, Canned Heat, Big Brother And The Holding Company, the association, Ravi Shankar, Hugh Masekela, Johnny Rivers, Quiksilver Messenger Service, Moby Grape, Al Kooper, Janis Joplin, Otis Redding, Electric Flag, Jefferson Airplane, The Blues Project, The Jimi Hendrix Experience, The Byrds, The Mamas & the Papas, laura nyro, The Butterfield Blues Band, Lou Rawls, Country Joe and the Fish, Paupers, The Group With No Name

It was May 1967 when I arrived in Monterey, California, driving my 1967 Austin Healey 3000 Mk3 British sports car. I had driven from Fort Rucker, Alabama, to Minden, Louisiana. From Minden, it was Highway 80 until I exited onto Highway 84 just west of Sweetwater, Texas, then to Route 66 in Amarillo, Texas. From Amarillo, I continued on Route 66 to Barstow, California. In Barstow, I exited onto Highway 58 to Highway 101, then Highway 101 to Salinas, and Highway 68 to Monterey.

Monterey Bay

Living in Seaside, which was adjacent to Monterey on the north, was someone who would be the girl of my dreams. It would be a few weeks before I met her, but when I did, I found she was everything I had ever dreamed of.

Not in my *wildest dreams*, however, did I think that ten years later, she would decide she no longer loved me - if she ever did. One of the first things she did after we were married was to throw away all of the love letters I had saved that she had written to me while I was in flight school and Vietnam. I guess she was getting rid of the evidence.

Most people enter marriage in the hopes that it will last forever. I know I did. When I married her, I knew it would be perfect. I had married the perfect girl (she frequently reminded me of that after we were married), I had great in-laws (I really did!), and we were both Christians!

It is said that on the night of their honeymoon, the man thinks, *"I hope this never changes,"* while the woman thinks about *"what she is going to change."* I know why the man thinks what he thinks! But why is the woman thinking about what she wants to change about him?

THINGS WERE GOING GREAT. Life was good. There had been no fights, major disagreements, or slow decay. Just a flick of the wrist and our marriage was flushed down the toilet. My rose-colored glasses had been yanked from my face. She had stopped any expressions of love for me.

When I asked her what was wrong, she would say, *"Nothing,"* or *"Everything is fine."* But, "things" obviously were not "fine." She had stopped loving me. Nothing hurts more than knowing the one you love no longer loves you. After this had gone on for several days, I told her how much it was hurting me. *Her response was to laugh at me!* My "Summer of Love" had ended.

But where could I go while waiting to fall out of love with her? I bought books on marriage and relationships, trying to discover what I'd done wrong. The Christian values and views I'd held my entire life about loyalty, commitment, and women had been turned upside down. The script of my life had been stolen and replaced with that piece of crap.

So, I turned to another woman. What should have felt like infidelity didn't. I had prayed endlessly for God to heal my marriage, but He didn't. I thought, *"If God doesn't care, why should I?"* Then it happened. My wife wanted me back. Not, apparently, because she realized she still loved me. She never said those words. It was because of *"what others would think."* But I'm getting ahead of myself.

CHAPTER 4
ARMY FLIGHT TRAINING

Fall, 1967 - Spring, 1968

The first phase of flight training was in "beefed-up" 172 Cessnas at Ft. Stewart, Georgia. In 1967, the Cessna Aircraft Company manufactured the Cessna T-41B Mescalero for the U.S. Army. It was also used by the United States Air Force and the armed forces of various other countries as a pilot training aircraft.

T-41Bs on the ramp at Hunter Field, Georgia

The US Army version, the T-41B, was a single-engine, high-wing aircraft with a 210 hp Continental IO-360 and constant-speed propeller in place of the 145 hp Continental O-300 and 7654 fixed-pitch propellers used in the 172 and the T-41A.

The need for more aviators because of the Vietnam conflict led to the response and expansion of the U.S. Army Aviation School at Fort Rucker, Alabama, which was expanded to Fort Stewart, Georgia, in 1967. When the Air Force closed its base at Hunter Field near Savannah in 1967, the Army promptly took control of the flight training. Fort Stewart, to the west, served as part of the training area.

Flight training consisted of flying half of the day and taking aviation, meteorology, and other flight-related classes the other half.

Cessna T-41B in a cow pasture

While flying, the student pilot continually looked for a place to land, usually a cow pasture. The instructor pilot would try to distract the student by pretending to be looking out his window or some other activity. If he thought the student wasn't paying attention, he would reach over and pull the throttle back, simulating an engine failure. The student would then set the aircraft up for landing and, if he had done it right, would land in a cow pasture or on a deserted dirt road. Most days, we returned to our home airfield, Hunter Field, with cow crap splattered all over the aircraft.

The Army T-41B was a great little aircraft. There were good reasons those who flew it nicknamed it Mescalero. The T-41Bs were tough birds. The T-41B flew circles around the regular Cessna 172 trainers. It is not that much faster, but it had a great rate of climb and easily got us out of short, unimproved fields.

T-41B beside a single-lane dirt road

UPON COMPLETING the initial phase of flight training, which lasted four months, we progressed to the multi-engine phase of flight training at Ft. Rucker, Alabama. During this training phase, we flew the Beechcraft Baron, a small twin-engine aircraft, flying out of Cairns Army Airfield, and became multi-engine qualified and instrument-rated.

Beechcraft Baron T-42 Cochise

ALMOST ALL OUR flights were cross-country, much of it "under the hood," landing at Athens, Georgia; Miami, Florida; Orlando, Florida; Birmingham, Alabama; and the Naval Air Station in Meridian, Mississippi. Shooting an approach and landing at Athens or Miami were experiences that were not soon forgotten.

What it looks like when the instructor is simulating an engine failure.

Approach control would give you an airspeed that might be substantially above what you would typically have flown on final approach, as they had fit you in between commercial airliners that were on approach for landing. You haven't lived until you glance over to your left on final approach and see a Boeing 707 or DC-8 on short final beside you. Once you touched down, faster than usual, you hauled butt to exit at the first taxiway to clear the runway for the airliner on short final to land behind you!

MIDWAY through the multi-engine phase of flight training, I had the opportunity, along with my flight instructor, to fly a DC-3 to Melbourne International Airport, Florida. The purpose of the flight was to take those of us who had invested in residential property at Port Malabar, Florida, to see our purchases and reassure us that we didn't need a glass-bottom boat to see it.

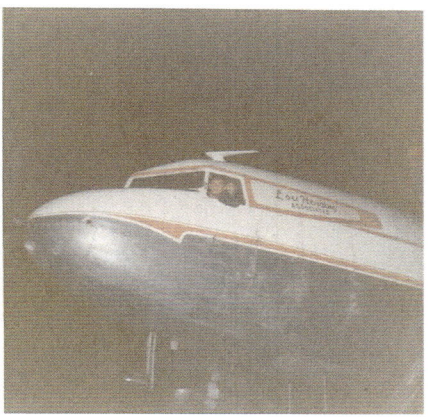

Lou Herring's DC-3

There were 25 to 30 passengers on board who must have had to go to the bathroom a lot, or were just walking back and forth visiting. Either way, the plane was constantly out of trim, keeping me busy with the trim wheel between the pilot and copilot seats.

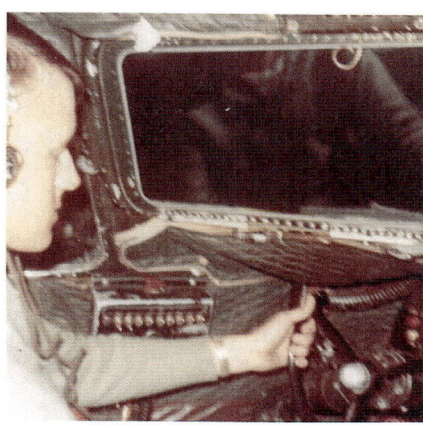

Passage leading to the cockpit

Upon landing in Melbourne, we were bussed to the Neptune Inn Resort on the Atlantic side of the Intracoastal Waterway (Indian River) south of Cocoa Beach. It was an older inn, and we were the only ones using it.

My flight instructor, visiting with Lou. He's the short one.

That first evening, after we all had settled in, they built a big bonfire on the beach, and there were free drinks and food, including a large barrel of iced-down oysters we had brought with us. I don't know what anyone else had to eat, but it was raw oysters for me!

Flying the DC-3 was an interesting experience, but I wouldn't want to fly one as a full-time occupation. I prefer something smaller and more quickly responsive.

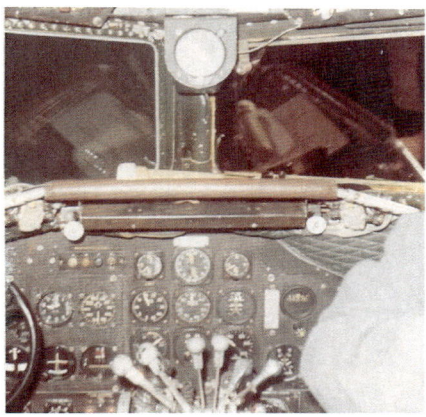

DC-3 Cockpit

I was a passenger on the return flight.

・ ・ ・

IN EARLY 1968, we were in the last two months of flight training. We were learning to fly the O-1 Bird Dog, the aircraft most of us would be flying in Vietnam. "Bird Dog" refers to its ability to seek out and locate the enemy on the ground. At the beginning of the Vietnam War, the L-19 was used primarily for observation and forward air control missions, so it became the O-1 (O for observation).

O-1 Bird Dog

The L-19A, designated the 0-1 Bird Dog in 1962, was the first all-metal, high-wing, single-engine, "fixed-wing" aircraft used by the US Army. It had dual controls for the pilot and the observer, who sat behind the pilot.

O-1 Bird Dog Cockpit

A Bird Dog pilot would locate and identify a target, then destroy it using artillery, helicopter gunships, or attack aircraft from the Air Force, Navy, and, occasionally, the Marines. The pilot used white phosphorus rockets on the Bird Dog to mark the target for gunships or attack aircraft. Afterward, the Bird Dog pilot would fly low over the target to make a "bomb damage assessment" or BDA. Enemy troops had good reason to fear the little Bird Dog.

About midway through our training, as we returned to Ft. Rucker from one of our staging airfields, one of the aircraft crashed. We were flying at 1,500 feet, with two students in each aircraft. I was flying third in the line of aircraft when I observed the flaps on the first Bird Dog begin lowering until they were in the full flap-down position. The nose of the plane pitched up; it stalled, spun in, crashed, and burned.

The student flying the plane ahead of me radioed, *"Oh my God! The plane in front of me just crashed! And it's burning!"* Except for a memorial service, I don't recall much being said by flight training personnel about the crash and loss of two lives.

I Got My Wings and New 1st Lieutenant Bars

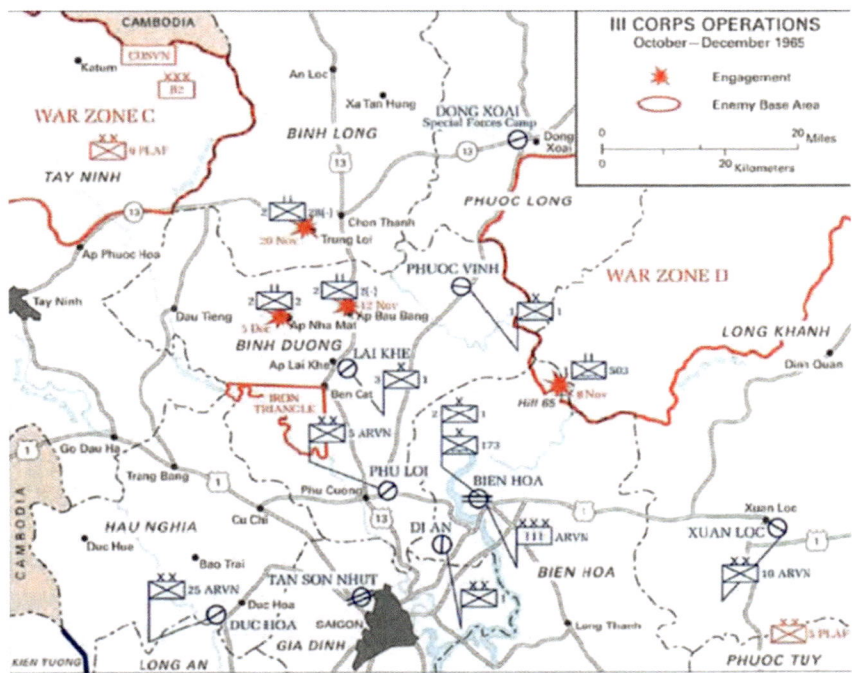

III Corps Operations in late 1965. The Michelin Rubber Plantation is near Dau Tieng. (U.S. Army)

CHAPTER 5
WELCOME TO VIETNAM

June - 1968

After completing flight training, I had a short leave, then departed Travis Air Force Base, California, en route to Vietnam via one of Braniff International's colorful aircraft. We flew into Biên Hòa, and on our approach to land, I looked out my window to the left and saw columns of black smoke rising from several areas of Saigon. It was beginning to sink in that this could be an unpleasant period of my life. It was 8 June 1968.

Biên Hòa Airfield

After we landed, I was transported to Long Binh in the back of a "deuce and a half" full of other arriving soldiers, for "in-country" processing. One of the pilots from the 74th Aviation Company (later changed to the 74th Recon Airplane Company or 74th RAC) picked me up the next day and flew me in one of the Bird Dogs to Phú Lợi, where our company was located. Phú Lợi is north of Saigon and west/northwest of Biên Hòa.

Long Binh

The following day, I was taken on my orientation flight. I have little memory of it except that my pilot and another Bird Dog pilot decided to play "dog fight," at which point I got sick and threw up out the window!

Aloft 24

Other than showing me some key geographical points, I was not given any in-country training. I was given the callsign "Aloft 24" (pronounced "two-four") and cleared for combat missions. My first missions were with an experienced "observer," usually from one of the artillery units. I tried to absorb as much as I could from them. After that, it was pretty much OJT.

During the first week that I was in Phú Lợi, we came under a heavy rocket and mortar attack one night. While running to a bunker, I sustained a minor cut to my left hand. I never figured out how it happened, but it was so trivial that I didn't report it.

G-2 Observer

ONE DAY, I PICKED UP AN "OBSERVER" from G-2 at Biên Hòa Air Field. We were assigned to check out an area east of Long Binh on the east/southeast side of a small stream that ran generally from the northeast to the southwest and eventually into the Đồng Nai River. We weren't told what to look for; at least I wasn't told.

We were flying at 800 to a thousand feet, just under a low cloud base. I passed over a small circular clearing with a single tree in the center. Sitting at the base of the tree was an individual dressed in black pajamas, cradling what appeared to be an AK-47 in his arms. The man was gone when I turned to fly back over the clearing.

I called the 105 battery at Long Binh and got clearance for a fire mission. After adjusting the first rounds to the target, I called the artillery battery to "fire for effect," firing five rounds at a time. I adjusted the rounds southwest along the east side of the stream for several hundred yards. After calling for a cease-fire, I flew over the area for a BDA. We had uncovered a vast bunker complex and observed bodies lying around. We received some ground fire but took no hits.

Bunker Complex

Australian and American units conducted a sweep of the area, and we were later advised that the bunker complex was a large, underground city, including a hospital! My observer and I thought we might have gotten some recognition for that find, but nah! Not even an "Atta Boy"! At least, nothing for me.

• • •

ONE OF MY extra duties was Pay Officer. It was my responsibility to fly to Tan Son Nhut in Saigon to pick up the money (actually MPC—military payment certificates) to pay indigenous personnel, which included the hooch maids, for their services to the 74th RAC in Phú Lợi.

Hooch Maids - All were Vietnamese except for the one using my left leg as an armrest. She was from Cambodia.

MPCs

CHAPTER 6
ON THE JOB TRAINING

For the next month, I flew missions in most of the southern III Corps area, during which time I had several "close calls." Since many of our daytime missions required flying "low and slow," the chances of being shot at were pretty good.

Most FAC missions were devoted to visual reconnaissance, which involved flying around looking for signs of enemy presence: fresh trails, new bunkers, smoke from campfires in uninhabited areas, unusually high volume of sampans on the waterways, etc. Constant monitoring of your assigned Area of Operation allowed the FAC to become familiar with "how things looked" from one day to the next. Any variations could then be seen, as Bird Dog pilots operated much as the scouts did back in the horse and wagon days of the Old West. To accomplish an effective recon, you had to fly low and slow, which varied depending on the terrain, noting any changes that had taken place.

By constantly patrolling the same area, FACs became familiar with the terrain and learned to detect any alterations that could indicate enemy forces hiding below. The triple-canopy jungles easily hid enemy troop movements. However, by 1968, FAC visual recon had largely suppressed daytime communist activities.

SOME DAYS WERE A LITTLE BORING. On one of those seemingly pointless reconnaissance missions of "boring holes in the air" over an endless triple-canopy jungle, I decided to do a low-level recon of the Đồng Nai River. It begins life in the central highlands of South Vietnam, northwest of Da Lat, and flows west and southwest for about 300 miles, joining the Saigon River southwest of Biên Hòa. I would be reconning an area of the river northwest of Biên Hòa.

I dropped down over the river, flying below treetop level to see under the trees. Now, I can see what's down here! I see women doing laundry and small children playing in the river, some waving at me, but no VC. After a few minutes, I climbed back up to my original 1,500-foot altitude.

Getting ready to low-level along the Dong Nai River

A few days later, another of our pilots, also last name Wilson, decided to low-level along the Saigon River northwest of Củ Chi and got the crap shot out of him. His Bird Dog was full of holes from the cockpit to the tail. Lt. Wilson took two rounds in his left arm but was able to make a safe landing at Củ Chi. His observer, an artillery captain, exited the plane as soon as it stopped and ran as fast as his short, chubby legs could carry him. I guess he wasn't injured. He always bragged about having a PhD, so all the pilots called him Captain Phud.

I didn't low-level along the river anymore. There were plenty of "hunter/killer teams" (LOH-6s and Cobras) for that. The LOH-6 would fly low-level, and when they stirred something up, the Cobra, flying along at a higher altitude, would roll in and open fire on it.

Once, while flying westbound along the Saigon River southwest of Lai Khê, a call came over "Guard" channel of *"heavy artillery from 30 thousand feet,"* and a set of coordinates was given. I checked my map and saw that I was flying directly over those coordinates! I made a hard left turn, pushed my throttle full forward, and headed away from the area. As I looked back over my shoulder at the ground, I saw long, double rows of eruptions barely past the tail of my aircraft!

B-52 Arc Light mission over Vietnam

CHAPTER 7
LOW AND SLOW

O ften, to fly a mission effectively, we were required to get down low. Since we were already flying slow, about 90 knots, going low and slow opened all kinds of opportunities for unique and unplanned excitement.

Taken from a vehicle in a convoy I was covering

I received a call requesting that I fly cover for a convoy departing Lai Khê and traveling north on Highway 13 (also known as Thunder Road) to An Lộc. The convoy is not far from my present location, and

I head that way. Convoys are a favorite ambush target for the VC as they are vulnerable and carry munitions, fuel, and supplies.

As I arrived over the convoy, I dropped down to begin my low-level recon of the areas along either side of the highway. Highway 13 has been cleared out to about one hundred yards on either side, but Charlie is an expert at camouflage and can lie in a shallow depression or "spider hole" covered by a woven grass mat without being seen. Today, there is no ambush. I'm getting low on gas, so I land at Lai Khê to refuel before continuing my recon.

I also flew cover for convoys on Highway 1 between Long Binh Post and Xuân Lộc and the highway between Dầu Tiếng and Tây Ninh.

ONE MORNING, I flew to Lai Khê to pick up a passenger. There was a low cloud cover that day, and as I neared Lai Khê, the clouds were almost at tree-top level. Approaching from the south was a rubber tree plantation extending almost to the south end of the runway. As the photo shows, a road passed through the plantation at a slight dog-leg from the runway.

Lai Khê Base Camp

Visibility was clear beneath the clouds, and there was sufficient distance between the rubber trees on either side of the road, so I radioed the tower that I would be flying low-level down the road to the runway. The tower replied that there was no other traffic and that I was cleared to land. I flew just a few feet above the road until I cleared the rubber trees, then banked to my right and landed. You do what you have to do.

CHAPTER 8
TAKING FIRE

Củ Chi Base Camp was established in 1966 near Highway 1, 15.5 miles northwest of Tan Son Nhut Air Base and 31 miles southeast of Tây Ninh. The camp was located south of the Vietcong stronghold known as the Iron Triangle and was near and, in some cases, above the Củ Chi Tunnels.

In order to combat better-supplied American and South Vietnamese forces during the Vietnam War, the Viet Cong (VC) dug tens of thousands of miles of tunnels, including an extensive network running underneath the Củ Chi district northwest of Saigon.

Communist forces began digging a network of tunnels under the jungle terrain of South Vietnam in the late 1940s during their war of independence from French colonial authority. As the United States escalated its military presence in Vietnam, North Vietnamese and Viet Cong troops gradually expanded the tunnels. At its peak, the network of tunnels in the Củ Chi district linked VC support bases over 155 miles, from the outskirts of Saigon to the Cambodian border.

. . .

ONE NIGHT, while flying in support of the 25th Infantry Division, I flew into Củ Chi to refuel. When I took off, thinking it would be safer to fly over Củ Chi village while gaining altitude, I was making a climbing left turn when red tracers started coming up all around me, "red tracers, not green!" The "enemy" uses green tracers. The sorry little bastards! I immediately turned off my navigation lights, made a hard right turn, and climbed for altitude! So much for friendly villages!

Củ Chi Base Camp

Then there was Spooky, or "Puff the Magic Dragon." Spooky was the first operational Air Force gunship. Armed with three side-firing 7.62mm miniguns, Spooky gunships dropped flares and stopped enemy ground attacks against airfields, bases, and villages. They also provided road convoy escort and close air support for troops in contact with the enemy. On thousands of occasions, Spooky crews prevented friendly ground positions from being overrun.

You don't want to mess with "Spooky"

Working with Spooky at night was an awesome experience. Observing such devastating firepower first-hand almost made you feel sorry for those on the receiving end—almost, but not quite. Mostly, everyone on our side was happy they were there when we needed them. Only every fifth round was a tracer!

Spooky at Night

ON SEVERAL OCCASIONS, while conducting low-level BDAs (Bomb Damage Assessments), I came under heavy fire! Many of our missions covered an area from Phu Cuong, on the Saigon River, northwest to Dầu Tiếng, west to Tây Ninh, north to "Snoopy's Nose" on the Cambodian border, and east to Phước Vĩnh. This area included the Micheline Rubber Plantation, Lai Khê, the Trapezoid, the Iron Triangle, and either side of Hwy. 1A north to Phước Vĩnh. I often came under fire while working in this area!

The Iron Triangle was a 120-square-mile area in the Bình Dương Province of Vietnam. It was named so because it was a stronghold of Việt Minh activity during the war.

The terrain within the Iron Triangle was flat, almost featureless, and covered by dense brush and undergrowth. The clearings, especially in the northern part, were thick with elephant grass, higher than a man's head. The surface was so scarred by countless bomb and shell craters that vehicular movement off the narrow, rough dirt roads was nearly impossible; even tracked vehicles had difficulty. There was a vast network of tunnels and trenches, most of them caved in and abandoned.

Its proximity to Saigon was a reason for both American and South Vietnamese efforts to eradicate it, as well as why it remained a crucial area for Communist forces to control.

CHAPTER 9
TÂY NINH

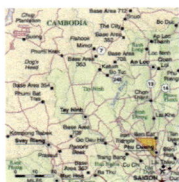

Tây Ninh Combat Base was established approximately 3 miles west of the city of Tây Ninh and 7.5 miles from the Vietnam-Cambodia border. Many of the day and night missions I flew were in and around this area.

Tây Ninh Combat Base

I also flew across the border into Cambodia a couple of times just to say, *"I flew in Cambodia,"* which we weren't supposed to do.

. . .

On 21 June 1969, after shelling it for two days, approximately 600 People's Army of Vietnam (NVA) soldiers stormed the US base near Tây Ninh. The Tây Ninh Combat Base, 50 miles northwest of Saigon, had been in operation since April 1966, where it served as the base for the 196th Light Infantry Brigade.

NVA forces launched six attacks on Tây Ninh city and the surrounding villages, displacing roughly 1,000 civilians as allied and communist troops fought in the city streets. NVA forces were eventually repulsed, suffering 194 known dead. U. S. casualties were light in comparison with 10 soldiers KIA.

The U. S. victory was an important one. In April 1970, Tây Ninh Combat Base was used as a staging area for U. S. units participating in the Cambodian Campaign for attacks west into the Parrot's Beak and north into the Fish Hook, areas on South Vietnam's border with Cambodia.

Captured enemy .51 caliber anti-aircraft gun silhouetted with Núi Bà Đen in the background at Tây Ninh Base Camp

Located 6.8 miles northeast of Tây Ninh, *Núi Bà Đen* rises 3,268 ft above the surrounding countryside's rice paddies and rubber plantations. Over the centuries, it has served as a shrine for various peoples of the area, including the Khmer, Cham, Vietnamese, and Chinese, and there are several interesting cave temples there.

The Mekong Delta is generally a flat region with the exception of the Black Virgin Mountain (*Núi Bà Đen*). The mountain commands everything in its sight and was, therefore, used as a staging area by both the Việt Minh and the VC, and was the scene of fierce fighting during the French and American Wars.

Núi Bà Đen

VARIATIONS of the legend of *Núi Bà Đen* exist. The oldest Khmer myth involves a female deity, "Neang Khmau," who left her footprints on the mountain rocks. The Vietnamese myth centers around a woman, *Bà Đen*, falling in love with a soldier, then, through betrayal or suicide, *Bà Đen* dies on the mountain. It has special significance to the Vietnamese Buddhist population and has a famous shrine about two-thirds of the way up the mountain. Also, to the Cao Dai sect, the mountain has special religious significance, and its temple, the Tây Ninh Holy See, is close to the mountain.

CHAPTER 10
XUÂN LỘC

After one month in Vietnam, I was transferred to Xuân Lộc, where I initially flew in support of MACV, then the 18th ARVN Division. I was also promoted to Captain.

During the nine months I was there, two of our pilots were killed in crashes due to "pilot error," and one due to hostile fire: Walter Fry. The two lost to "pilot error" were Ken Hughes and Jean Foster.

Hughes was involved in a mid-air collision at the west end of the Biên Hòa airfield, and Foster crashed just northeast of Xuân Lộc due to attempting an aerobatic maneuver from which he was too low to pull out.

Foster's Bird Dog

. . .

Just before Christmas 1968, I received a care package from my fiancé containing a round metal cookie tin with homemade "fruit cake" cookies. I dislike fruit cake in any form, so I placed the container of cookies on the bar, near the outside wall of our "officers' club," for anyone to eat.

That night, we came under heavy mortar and rocket attack. My hooch mate, Scott Rutherford, whose bunk was closest to the outside wall, hit the floor and crawled under his bunk. I stayed in mine, thinking that the sandbags around the outside of the building would prevent any shrapnel from entering high enough to hit me. I was wrong. Some small pieces came through above Scott's bed, and two hit my right arm. If Scott had stayed in his bunk, they would have hit him!

Mine and Scott's Hooch

As in Phú Lợi, I didn't report the injuries since they were just minor cuts. I didn't feel right receiving a Purple Heart for such minor injuries. Shrapnel had also come through the wall of our "officers' club," blowing holes in the cookie container and cookies! I guess Charlie didn't like fruit cake either!

GARY R. WILSON

Downtown Xuân Lộc

CHAPTER 11
A WING AND A PRAYER

"Wavy Leaf Alpha" was the call sign of an infantry lieutenant colonel at Xuân Lộc. I had visited with him on several occasions, but I can't remember his name. Late one afternoon, west/southwest of Xuân Lộc, I was flying convoy coverage for an infantry unit coming out of the jungle. Wavy Leaf Alpha was at the head of the convoy and had asked me to stay with them until they were onto the highway, as it was getting dark. As it got darker, they still weren't clear of the jungle, and I was getting low on fuel! I radioed Wavy Leaf Alpha and told him I was low on fuel and had to leave. He asked me not to leave until they had the highway in sight!

The fuel gauges on a Bird Dog are little, round, needle gauges activated by a float in the fuel tanks, which are in the wings next to the cockpit. When the gauges are showing empty, you can see if any fuel is left by rocking your wings to see if the needles bounce. My needles didn't bounce, and I was at least ten minutes from Xuan Loc. I saw Wavy Leaf Alpha's jeep emerge from the jungle, and I radioed to him that I was leaving, that I was out of fuel!

When I was about 5 minutes out, I radioed Xuân Lộc that I was approaching to land. That's when all hell broke loose! It looked like a 4th of July fireworks display! Rockets and mortars were going off all over the place; tracers were coming in and going out, then the big guns and mortars started firing out of Xuân Lộc!

The tower replied, *"Negative! We are under attack and are receiving heavy fire! Go to Blackhorse!"* Well, I didn't know how I was still flying as it was, and Blackhorse was another 15 minutes away! I told the tower that I was out of gas and was landing anyway, if I could make it that far! When I made the left turn onto short final to land, all the fireworks stopped as if someone had flipped a switch! I landed in total darkness and taxied to the parking ramp, where my engine died!

"It is the Lord
who goes before you. He will be with you;
He will not leave you or forsake you.
Do not fear or be dismayed." **(Deuteronomy 31:8)**

CHAPTER 12
OOPS AND CONGRATULATIONS

On one occasion, flying from Xuân Lộc to Phú Lợi, the Bird Dog I was flying was out of trim, causing it to fly one wing heavy, requiring constant opposite pressure on the stick. I had the fuel selector positioned to use fuel in that tank to lighten the wing.

As I was taking off for my return to Xuân Lộc, I had barely cleared the departure end of the runway when my engine died! I immediately kicked hard left rudder, shoved the stick to the left and forward, increased the degree of flaps, and landed safely back on the runway. I had forgotten to move my fuel selector from the empty tank to the full tank!

The tower operator asked me if I needed any assistance. I advised him that I didn't, as I selected the "full" fuel tank. I was a little shaken up as I taxied back down the runway. When in position, I received clearance for takeoff again and headed back to Xuân Lộc. After landing, I asked the crew chief to adjust the trim!

Battalion Party

ONE AFTERNOON, we had a battalion party in our compound at Xuân Lộc. After it had gotten dark, the infantry brigade commander, who had been flown up for the party, needed a ride back to Long Binh. I flew him back and, at his request, landed at the Long Binh Plantation Airfield.

Plantation Airfield is a very small airfield that runs slightly uphill. There is only one way in and one way out, as there are buildings sitting on an elevated area at the upper end. I was approaching from the north, and once I neared the airfield, I had to drop down to about 300 feet, fly south along a shallow valley, then bank to the right to line up with the runway. It was a very tricky approach for a fixed-wing aircraft, especially at night.

Plantation Airfield is noted in blue

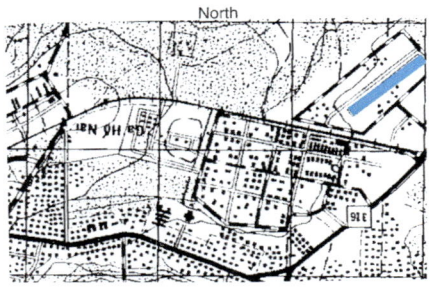

Plantation Airfield
(Noted in blue in the upper right corner)

After I landed and taxied up in front of the tower, one of the tower personnel ran out to my plane, handed me a bottle of Seagram's Seven Crown, and said, *"For being the first fixed-wing pilot with balls enough to land on our field at night!"* The colonel patted me on the shoulder and said, *"Congratulations. It looks like I had the right pilot for the job."*

After removing the label (to keep in memory of the occasion), I donated the booze to our officers' club. I still have the label.

CHAPTER 13
HÀM TÂN

Hàm Tân is a coastal village on the South China Sea, about 18.5 miles southeast of Phan Thiết and 105.5 miles from Saigon. I enjoyed the missions I flew in that area because it was beautiful and presented some very interesting sites: Buddha Mountain, Ke Ga Lighthouse, and the village of Hàm Tân, to name a few.

Buddha Mountain

There are two famous pagodas on the top of Ta Cu Mountain (known to us as Buddha Mountain): Linh Son Truong Tho Pagoda & Long Doan Pagoda. One of the most unique and biggest statues of Buddha in Southeast Asia reclines on its right side on Buddha Mountain. The statue, 160.9 feet in length and 36 feet in height, was made from reinforced concrete and covered with white lime on a stone base. It was built in 1962 and completed after nearly four years. Buddha Mountain was a VC stronghold and R&R area.

Ke Ga Lighthouse

. . .

Ke Ga Lighthouse is located on Ke Ga Island, 984 feet offshore of the mainland (of South Vietnam), which belongs to Tân Thành Commune, Hàm Thuận Nam District, Bình Thuận Province. It is the tallest and oldest lighthouse in Southeast Asia.

Ke Ga Island, also called Hòn Bà, covers *12.35 acres* with hundreds of huge blocks of granite and 100-year-old Su (Plumeria) trees.

According to lighthouse keepers on Ke Ga Island, in the late 19th century, Ke Ga Island was considered to be in a very important position because ships had difficulty navigating the sea route from Phan Rang to Vũng Tàu. Many boats and ships crossing the area sank because they could not define their coordinates and position. To ensure the safety of transport ships of French troops and foreign merchant ships, the French built a big lighthouse on the island in 1897. It was completed in 1899 and was put into operation in 1900.

Designed by a French architect, Ke Ga Lighthouse is 213 feet 3 inches high and has a 114-foot granite lamp tower. Granite blocks were carefully shaped to fit in each position. During construction, the stones were correctly placed in position using mortar. The top of the tower uses a 2000 W lamp with an effective radius of 22 nautical miles or 40 km.

Inside the tower, a steel spiral staircase with 183 steps leads to the top. The staircase, dynamo, and lamp were imported from France.

At the foot of the tower is a concrete road leading down to the bottom of the hill. Both sides of the road are shaded all year round by two rows of old Su (Plumeria) trees planted by the French when construction of the lighthouse began.

Despite the impact of wind, waves, and typhoons, the 125-year-old Ke Ga lighthouse still stands without damage.

. . .

Since "light" is a symbol of Christianity, lighthouses have a special meaning. They represent the guidance, hope, and salvation that were fulfilled in the life of Christ. John 12:46 says, *"I [Jesus] have come into the world as a light, so that no one who believes in Me should stay in darkness."*

Hàm Tân with Buddha Mountain in the background

CHAPTER 14
R&R
MY RIDE TO CAMRON BAY WHERE I WOULD CATCH THE FREEDOM BIRD TO JAPAN.

U-6A De Havilland Beaver

During the year I was in Vietnam, I had two one-day in-country R&Rs and one out-of-country R&R. The first in-country R&R was to Vũng Tàu on the South China Sea, and I flew one of the Bird Dogs to that one.

The beach at Vũng Tàu

Although I was driven through the village of Vũng Tàu, I spent the day on the beach. I did, however, take some pictures.

Downtown Vũng Tàu

My next in-country R&R was to Saigon. My friend Scott Rutherford and I commandeered a jeep for our one-day jaunt. That's it at the bottom left of the picture.

I'll refrain from any commentary for the rest of this one-day vacation, so enjoy the pictures.

GARY R. WILSON

Downtown Saigon

Freedom Bird

For my out-of-country R&R, I chose Japan for several reasons. The first, and most important at the time, was that the young lady I was engaged to was half Japanese, and I was supposed to meet her mother's side of the family. That would have been very interesting and culturally enlightening, except that I chickened out and didn't meet with them. That is one of the many regrets I have had in my life.

The second reason I chose Japan was that I was genuinely interested in touring Japan, enjoying the food, and soaking up its ambiance.

The third was that I wanted to shop for stereo equipment. I accomplished everything while I was on R&R, except the first and most important one.

CHAPTER 15
MEDALS AND DOUBTS

On 4-5 February 1969, while flying in support of a company of the 18th ARVN Division northeast of Xuân Lộc, I was advised that they were in contact with an enemy unit and were taking heavy fire. In this area, ground units have no direct radio contact for support and rely on us, the "Aloft" pilots, for all their needs. I was Aloft 24.

They popped smoke, enabling me to locate the ARVN unit. By making several low passes over the area, I was able to accurately locate the enemy unit. The American adviser started yelling at me, *"Get your ass out of there! You're taking fire!"* So I did! That isn't the safest way to locate the enemy, but sometimes, it's the only way. While waiting for Air Force "fast movers" (close air support) to arrive, I called in artillery support from the 155 battery at Blackhorse and an 8-inch gun at Xuân Lộc.

THE NEXT DAY, the ARVN unit was again in heavy contact with an enemy unit of unknown size. After the friendly unit popped smoke and advised their position in relation to the enemy unit, I again accurately located the enemy unit by making low passes. The American adviser again advised me that I was taking heavy fire and to take evasive action!

After calling for helicopter gunships, I again called in artillery support until the gunships arrived on station. When the gunships arrived, I rolled in, marked the target with one of my WP marking rockets, and gave the gunship pilots instructions for making their rocket runs.

Their first two passes went well, but the next couple of runs were putting fire on friendlies. Both the American adviser and I were calling the gunships to cease fire — that they were hitting friendlies, but there was no response from the gunships. As they were lining up for another run, I rolled over and dropped down to fly across in front of them, rocking my wings and calling, *"Cease fire, cease fire"!* That time, they "rogered" and broke off their rocket run.

Huey Gunship

I IMMEDIATELY RECEIVED a request for Medevac from the ground unit. I called for the Medevac, and after they arrived, I continued to fly command and control coverage for the ground unit. I watched the Medevac Huey hover just above the triple-canopy jungle, being directed to where a jungle penetrator could be lowered to extract the wounded.

Dustoff

The medevac was hovering slowly to its right when I saw it start to wobble. It then rolled to its left and crashed upside down into the jungle, bursting into flames! It suddenly felt like I was in a dream where everything was going in slow motion. I was just flying around and around, and felt detached from the events taking place. I knew I was getting low on fuel, but I didn't want to leave. Maybe, if I stayed long enough, there would be a happy ending — one without the death of that Dustoff crew.

I felt I had failed those guys on the ground and those in that medevac chopper. I've always felt guilty and second-guessed myself about the events of that second day. Did I do something that caused injuries to the ground troops and cost the lives of the medevac crew? Did I misdirect the gunships? I never sleep well at night and have nightmares and flashbacks of those events.

I received the Distinguished Flying Cross and the Vietnamese Cross of Gallantry for my actions during those two days, but I never felt I deserved them. I made it home to be with family and friends. They didn't!

CHAPTER 16
NIGHT FLYING

After nine months at Xuân Lộc, I went back to Phú Lợi for my last two months "in country," where I mainly flew night missions. I flew a total of 1309 combat hours during my year in Vietnam — 324 at night. Some of those missions were night mortar/rocket watch missions at Tây Ninh, Dầu Tiếng, Lai Khê, or Biên Hòa. Other missions were flying in support of Long Range Reconnaissance Patrol teams or LRRPs (pronounced "lurps"). Flying at night may not sound like a big deal, but a Bird Dog has no navigational instruments, and there are no lights out in the boonies by which to guide.

Night Flying

I began flying more night missions out of Dầu Tiếng, Lai Khê, and Tây Ninh. We tried different tactics, none of which worked very well. We would either fly around looking for flashes of a rocket taking off or of mortar rounds leaving a tube, or sit on the ground until we had incoming, then take off and try to spot them.

One night, while flying just east of Biên Hòa, a huge shadow blocked the sky above and in front of me. I immediately turned right and down, leveled out, looked back up, and saw the running lights of a C-130 come on. He was flying, at night, near a large airfield, without his navigation lights on!

Another night, while flying night mortar/rocket watch north northeast of Biên Hòa, huge green tracers came up past the left front of my aircraft, so close that they lit up the inside of my cockpit! I immediately turned off "my" running lights and made a hard right turn! *"Hello, Biên Hòa! You have a 51 caliber anti-aircraft gun out here!"*

On one night mission at Dầu Tiếng, we started receiving heavy incoming while waiting in a building near the flight line. I had jumped in a jeep with the driver to take me out to my plane when the incoming fire stopped, and we saw black-clad figures running in the distance!

Dầu Tiếng (runway is at the top of the photo)

We both jumped out of the jeep and into the ditch beside the road, where I tried to become part of the dirt! Several people wearing black pajamas ran by the jeep, and one threw something in it, then they all took off! We lay in the ditch for what seemed like hours until friendly troops cleared the area. Seeing what had been thrown in the jeep made me weak in the knees (as if they weren't weak enough already). It was a satchel charge that had not gone off! (A satchel charge is essentially several kilos of explosives packed together, usually inside a special case or bag (hence its name) or taped or tied together.)

> *"Fear not, for I am with you;*
> *be not dismayed, for I am your God;*
> *I will strengthen you, I will help you,*
> *I will uphold you with my righteous right hand."*
> **(Isaiah 41:10)**

About two months before I went home (I think it was in April), a new pilot arrived: Thom De Palma. As I noted earlier, I began flying almost all "night missions" after I returned to Phú Lợi. About a month before I went home, Thom was assigned to fly night missions. I gave Thom his night orientation briefing and night orientation flight. He then flew with me on a night mission, and on another night, I flew in the back seat on his first night mission.

That night, we were making lazy circles north of Biên Hòa, looking for mortars or rockets, when we began flying in and out of low clouds at the east end of our orbit. Wanting to see how Thom would deal with the situation, I didn't say anything. With each circle, we flew farther and farther into the cloud until we were entirely in it.

Thom finally keyed his mike and told me something was wrong with the instruments. He had gotten vertigo, also known as spatial disorientation, and his inner ear was telling him that the instruments weren't reading correctly. I calmly told him there was nothing wrong with the instruments, that he was experiencing vertigo, and that he should reduce altitude until we were out of the cloud. He did, and the rest of the night was uneventful. After that flight, I signed him off as qualified to fly night missions.

A FEW NIGHTS LATER, on 22 May 1969, Thom was coming in to land at Phú Lợi when the tower told him to make a 360-degree turn and set up his approach behind another plane that was landing with a "VIP" on board. While Thom was making his 360-degree turn so the "VIP" could land, he was shot down and killed. The "VIP" was Colonel George S. Patton III. I have recently been in contact with the husband of Thom's daughter, a daughter whose daddy wasn't there to walk her down the aisle because a "VIP" couldn't wait for his turn to land, causing the death of another friend!

Thom De Palma

CHAPTER 17
GOING HOME

As I neared the end of my tour in Vietnam, I received orders for my next duty assignment. The Army has what is called "dream sheets," on which an officer can select three choices of where he would like to be sent. I had submitted a dream sheet with my choices of (1) Ft. Ord, California, (2) Ft. Carson, Colorado, and (3) Ft. Hood, Texas. The Army rarely, if ever, honors any of the selections, hence the name "dream sheet."

When I received the orders for my new duty station, all it said was "APO Seattle, Washington." What the heck was APO Seattle, Washington? I asked around and was told that I was going to Alaska! Alaska?! I didn't want to go to Alaska!

I was going to call my Branch Officer to try and convince him to get me to one of my dream sheet's locations when one of our pilots, Pop Blanchfield, stopped me and told me I would love Alaska. So, I went to Alaska, and "I loved it!"

In memory of Robert "Pop" Blanchfield. Pop passed in 2014 at 82 years of age.

Robert "Pop" Blanchfield joined the U.S. Air Force when he was 17 and served as a tail gunner on B-29s in the Korean War. He wanted to fly, so he received a branch transfer to the army, where he earned his wings and served two tours in Vietnam. After 21 years of service, he retired from the Army as a CWO3.

CHAPTER 18
ALASKA

The late 1940s saw a transition from the World War II Japanese threat in the North Pacific region to another threat by Soviet bombers. Alaska became an air theater of operations, and senior commanders were assigned from the ranks of Air Force generals.

The Soviets had developed a four-engine, long-range bomber capable of delivering nuclear weapons to Northwestern United States targets on one-way flights from Arctic staging bases near Alaska. The bomber's range could be extended farther by capturing forward bases in Alaska. This resulted in the construction of an extensive aircraft control and warning system with radar stations located on Alaska's periphery and interior, which was later augmented by the Alaska Segment of the Distant Early Warning (DEW) Line.

Based out of Elmendorf AFB near Anchorage and Ladd AFB near Fairbanks, fighter interceptors were maintained on 15-minute alert at King Salmon and Galena forward bases. The main bases provided command and control, logistics support, and housed the ground forces.

While the emphasis during World War II had been on perimeter defenses, the forces were now concentrated around the main bases of Elmendorf AFB and Fort Richardson near Anchorage, Ladd AFB (later Fort Wainwright) near Fairbanks, Eielson AFB east of Fairbanks, and the Navy base on Kodiak Island. The military mission in Alaska centered on maintaining deterrence against Soviet aggression and providing a training environment for Arctic and cold region warfare.

THAT's where I was headed in July 1969. Between my Vietnam and Alaska tours, I had about a month's leave and travel time with a lot of stuff to do, the first of which was to get married for the first time. I was married in Seaside, California, the hometown of my first ex-wife. We went to Hawaii for our honeymoon, which was pretty cool. From there, we were on our way to Alaska via Abilene, Texas; Minden, Louisiana; Twin Falls, Minnesota; Yellowstone National Park; and Seattle, Washington.

After dropping my car off to be shipped to Anchorage, my new wife and I boarded an Alaska Airlines flight to Fairbanks and my new duty assignment at Fort Wainwright.

Fort Wainwright. Our hangar is circled in red.

Fort Wainwright is adjacent to Fairbanks, shown at the upper edge of the image. Fairbanks is the second-largest city in Alaska, located 365 miles north of Anchorage. Alaska's housing and other living expenses were much higher than in the Lower 48 states. A 10-cent cup of coffee in the Lower 48 was 50 cents in Alaska.

The weather in that area of Alaska has the largest swings in the world. It can reach temperatures of 90 degrees or higher in the summer and as low as -65 degrees in the winter. It reached -72 degrees while I was there, and I flew a mission in the U-1A De Havilland Otter with the temperature at -65 degrees at takeoff. On the plus side, it boasts breathtaking scenery, beautiful mountains, diverse wildlife, and excellent opportunities for hunting, fishing, and camping.

Fishing for Lake Trout on Summit Lake with my friend, Larry Smithee

ALASKA HAS A VERY complex aviation environment. Flying safely requires thorough planning and special attention. When properly planned, flying in Alaska presents some of the most inspiring, interesting, and adventurous experiences in aviation. Summer flying weather is generally good with long daylight hours.

Much of Alaska is mountainous. The correct entrance to mountain passes can be deceptive, and dead-end valleys are common. Updrafts and downdrafts often present unexpected and dangerous conditions when flying in the mountains. Magnetic variation may be as much as 25 degrees east.

Icing conditions can occur year-round, though they are less prevalent in the summer. Most of Alaska's runways are gravel, and many are not lighted. Airspace around major population centers can be pretty crowded and contain special restrictions and requirements.

A pilot may not fly an aircraft in the State of Alaska unless emergency equipment is carried as follows:

1. The minimum equipment during the summer months is food for each occupant for one week, one axe or hatchet, one first aid kit, an assortment of fishing tackle such as hooks, flies, and sinkers, one

knife, a fire starter, one mosquito head net for each occupant, and two signaling devices such as colored smoke bombs, pistol shells, etc. sealed in metal containers.

2. In addition to the above, the following must be carried as minimum equipment from October 15 to April 1 of each year: one pair of snowshoes, one sleeping bag, and one wool blanket for each occupant over four years of age. Army aircraft carried two Arctic sleeping bags and a 410 single-shot, breakdown shotgun, along with the other survival gear.

U-1A De Havilland Otter with Skis
The U-1A Otter is powered by a 600 hp Pratt & Whitney R-1340 Twin Wasp radial piston engine. It can reach a maximum speed of 160 mph and has a cruise speed of 138 mph.

FLYING in Alaska really is different. Weather, terrain, extreme temperatures, 24-hour periods of daylight or darkness, vast areas without radar or radio coverage, and rough, rugged airstrips make Alaska a uniquely challenging and rewarding place to fly. These extreme conditions require special training, self-reliance, and a way of thinking that's a little different from the Lower 48. Military pilots were also required to complete an Arctic Aircrew Survival Course.

During my two years in Alaska, I flew the extreme limits of the state and into western Canada. From Kodiak Island in the southeast, Cold Bay in the southwest, Kenai and Anchorage in the south, Nome, Bethel, and Tin City in the west, Saint Lawrence Island in the extreme west, Kotzebue in the northwest, Barrow in the north, Ft. Greely and Summit in the east, and Eagle Village and Fort Yukon on the Yukon River, I flew missions over most of the state.

I FLEW the U-1A De Havilland Otter and the O-1 Bird Dog, making takeoffs and landings on wheels and skis. I also flew the U-21A Ute, a twin-engine turboprop, flying many AI (actual instrument) missions.

The L-19A, designated the O-1 Bird Dog in 1962, is an all-metal, high-

wing aircraft powered by a 213-horsepower engine. It has dual controls for the pilot and the observer, who sits behind the pilot. The almost 360-degree visibility from the cockpit made it ideal for observation, control, and reconnaissance.

The U-21A Ute is powered by two Pratt & Whitney PT6A-20 engines, each rated at 550 hp. Most U-21As eventually served with the U.S. Army in Southeast Asia.

PILOTS TALK about all types of flying, but when you mention flying in Alaska, they look at you like you forgot to lower your landing gear. Flying in Alaska can be as fun and safe as in other remote areas if you familiarize yourself with the flying environment and use common sense. It was a fun and exciting adventure to fly in Alaska.

 # Fairbanks
Daily News-Miner

"America's Farthest North Daily Newspaper" — Member of The Associated Press

Vol. LXXVII — 10c Per Copy — FAIRBANKS, ALASKA, TUESDAY, MARCH 2, 1971 — Eighteen Pages — NO. 51

142.2 inches of snow; wow that's heavy!

Surpasses record depth of 1936-37

BY BIX LEWIS
Staff Writer

It had to happen and did—total snowfall this winter has finally reached and passed the record total for a whole winter's snowfall.

The National Weather Service reported this morning that 142.2 inches of that white stuff that just keeps coming have fallen since September, beating the previous snow total of 134.5 inches set in the winter of 1936-37. Records have been kept by the weather service since 1906.

On the ground now is 43 inches of snow, including the official inches which fell Sunday, to beat the previous record. The water equivalent of the snow on the ground is 9.4 inches.

So far in the two days of March, 5.2 inches have fallen. Dan Sain, meteorologist in charge at NWS, said this morning that Fairbanks is in for a "little cold spell," with snow ending for a few days at least. But, said the system producing this storm is dissipating, and no more snow is expected through Thursday. Temperatures will be slightly colder.

Since this season began early in September, just only 4.1 inches fell that month. For the smaller monthly total this winter in October, 21.9 inches fell. November saw the largest monthly total, with 54 inches. In December, 32.5 inches fell. In January, only 9.3 inches of snow fell, but mixed now temperatures with not always dry, leaving almost no new snow to speak about. In February 19.1 inches fell.

Normal seasonal total for snowfall is 64.8 inches, a figure

passed this winter in mid November.

Because of the heavy snowfall, speculation is rampant on whether or not Fairbanks is in for a spring flood. Larry Mayo, of the Geological Survey, said this morning that the existing snow pack keeps on building, the generally obvious that it will be hard to shovel all that water through the little river that we have.

A meeting on flood possibilities was held yesterday by city officials, and another is scheduled by the University of Alaska's Institute of Water Resources for March 18. That meeting will be a symposium on flood hazards in connection with a possible flood, and will be conducted by Dr. Robert Carlson, associate professor of hydrology at UA.

CHAPTER 19
KENAI

The Kenai Peninsula was on fire. Greeting my arrival in Alaska was a fire on the Kenai Peninsula, known as the Swanson River fire, which burned about 80,000 acres. Flames raced across the dry spruce of the Kenai National Wildlife Refuge area in August 1969.

Recently checked out in the U-1A De Havilland Otter, I was tasked with flying supplies and firefighters into Kenai, Alaska. Thankfully, the major who was my instructor pilot for the Otter was flying with me, as I was still relatively new at flying it. We were making instrument approaches into Kenai due to the heavy smoke.

"USING the same overall configuration as the highly successful de Havilland Beaver (DHC-2), the Otter actually began life described as the King Beaver; longer, with a wider wingspan and far heavier, but capable of seating up to 11, the Otter was conceived simply as a big Beaver, able to fulfill the same functions. The aircraft features the same conventional stressed skin construction and has a braced wing with full-span slotted flaps, the outer portions acting as ailerons. The US Army was the largest

customer, taking delivery of 200 aircraft commencing in 1955." — **DHC-3 tribute website DHC3Otter.com**

U-1A De Havilland Otter

It took four thousand people to fight the Swanson River Fire, armies of heavy equipment, and nearly 80 bulldozers that surrounded the burn with 110 miles of fire line. Around 700,000 gallons of retardant were dropped.

Kenai Peninsula

In all my research to obtain detailed information about the fire, I found not one mention of the US Army's assistance in fighting it.

．．．

THE CITY of Kenai is named after the local Dena'ina word 'ken' or 'kena,' which means 'flat, meadow, open area with few trees; base, low ridge,' according to the Dena'ina Topical Dictionary by James Kari, Ph.D., published in 2007. This describes the area along the mouth and portion of the Kenai River near the City of Kenai. Archaeological evidence suggests that the area was first occupied by the Kachemak people from 1000 B.C. until they were displaced by the Dena'ina Athabaskan people around 1000 A.D. Before the arrival of the Russians, Kenai was a Dena'ina village called *Shk'ituk't*, meaning "where we slide down." When Russian fur traders first arrived in 1741, about 1,000 Dena'ina lived there. The traders called the people "Kenaitze," which is a Russian term for "people of the flats" or "Kenai people." This name was later adopted when they were incorporated as the Kenaitze Alaskan Natives in the early 1970s.

Kenai is the largest community on the Kenai Peninsula with a population of around 7,800. The city sits on a low rise overlooking the mouth of the Kenai River. To the west, majestic views of the Alaska Range and three active volcanoes (Mount Spurr, Mount Iliamna, and Mount Redoubt) make for a dramatic backdrop. Located on the western side of the Kenai Peninsula, the town of Kenai is 160 miles from Anchorage and 80 miles from Homer.

CHAPTER 20
KODIAK ISLAND

In late summer 1969, my copilot, CWO3 Darrell "Doc" Waters, and I, flying the U-21A, were assigned to pick up VIP passengers at the Naval base on Kodiak Island. While there, we ate lunch in the base dining hall. It was pleasant to dine in a military dining facility, which was more like a nice restaurant, and enjoy some local cuisine.

Kodiak Naval Air Station

Flying over Alaska at any time is a spectacular experience, but during the winter, it is even more so. The state's rugged beauty unfolds before you, a succession of white mountain peaks against pale blue skies, icy lakes, and frozen rivers that snake as far as the eye can see. It's an awesome sight, wild and pristine, that glows in a myriad of hues of red, orange, and pink when the sun sets beyond the horizon.

But you eventually have to land, and landing in Alaska can be.......interesting.

Surrounded by mountains, the approach to Juneau's airport is often buffeted by treacherous wind shear. Sitka's one small runway is on a narrow strip of land surrounded by water. At Fort Greely, buffalo are frequently on the runway, and it, too, is buffeted by treacherous winds coming off the Alaska Range.

Once, when landing at Fort Richardson in the U-21A, I had to use reverse props for braking and vary the pitch of the props for steering as the runway was covered with a sheet of ice.

In Kodiak, the landing strip ends abruptly at a mountainside with an approach to the airport that can be a little tricky.

Kodiak Naval Air Station with Barometer Mountain in the background.

I flew into Kodiak both during the summer and winter. You don't want to miscalculate, or you will hit a mountain. Landing at Kodiak is pretty much a one-shot deal. You land toward the mountains. You take off, going away from the mountains.

The famous Barometer Mountain is right at the end of runway

25! Shaped like a pyramid (Pyramid Mountain is actually across the valley to the north), Barometer Mountain is the subject of an old Kodiak weather joke. "That's Barometer Mountain. If there are no clouds around it, then it's about to rain. If there *are* clouds around it, then it *is* raining!" The joke won't win any comedy awards, but……. there it is.

THE RUNWAYS at Kodiak's main airport were built by the military in the run-up to World War II. Until the early 1970s, while under the Navy's control, they carried the designation NHB, which local lore said meant "Nice Hungry Bears." They should have kept that since it was a more interesting designation than ADQ.

Located 30 miles south of the Alaska Peninsula, Kodiak Island's landscape includes mountains, rivers, lakes, and oceanfront. The city of Kodiak is located on Kodiak Island. Known as the Emerald Isle, Kodiak Island is 3,670 square miles and more than 100 miles long. It is Alaska's largest island and the second-largest island in the United States.

THE ALUTIIQ/SUGPIAQ people have inhabited the Kodiak area for several thousand years. In the mid-1700s, a Russian explorer visited the island, ushering in its Russian period. Kodiak was Russian-controlled Alaska's first capital and an important location in the lucrative fur trade.

Once a struggling fishing port, World War II turned the island of Kodiak into a major staging area for North Pacific operations. At one point, Kodiak's population topped 25,000, with Fort Abercrombie built as a defense post to protect the naval base, which was constructed in 1939. Today, the old naval base is the site of the largest Coast Guard base in the country.

. . .

KODIAK ISLAND IS ALSO KNOWN for the Kodiak bears, also known as the Kodiak brown bear. These bears are a unique subspecies of the brown or grizzly bear (*Ursus arctos middendorffi*). They live exclusively on the islands in the Kodiak Archipelago and have been isolated from other bears for several thousand years.

Though Kodiak bears are often claimed as the world's largest land carnivores (meat eaters), they are really omnivores (eating a variety of foods).

CHAPTER 21
CARIBOU HUNTING

Fall 1969

My friend, CWO2 Larry Smithee, and I had observed large herds of Caribou while flying the U-1A De Havilland Otter in an area southwest of Eagle Village on the Yukon River. I had also seen them when flying to and from Fort Yukon on the northeast side of the river. While hanging out in the hangar one day with some of our NCOs, we told them about seeing the caribou herds. They asked if we could fly them to that area and drop them off for a few days to hunt Caribou. We put our heads together and came up with a plan.

A CARIBOU IS NOT JUST a caribou. The Boone and Crockett Club recognizes five subspecies in North America: the mountain, woodland, Alaska-Yukon barren-ground, Central Canada barren-ground, and Quebec-Labrador varieties.

In Europe, caribou are called reindeer, but in Alaska and Canada, only the semi-domesticated form is called reindeer. All caribou and reindeer worldwide are considered to be the same species, but there are five subspecies, including the Arctic Islands Caribou, formerly Peary Caribou, which are found on Saint Lawrence Island.

Alaska predominantly has barren-ground subspecies and one small herd of woodland caribou, the Chisana herd, which crosses into Canada in Southcentral Alaska's Wrangell-Saint Elias area.

Both bull and cow caribou carry antlers. Bulls wear impressive headgear—flaring, palmated antlers up to 5 feet long, adorned with large scoop-like brow tines called shovels that often extend out over the nose. Cow antlers are small and spindly, rarely reaching 2 feet in length.

ALL CARIBOU MIGRATE, moving between summering and wintering grounds. Sometimes, you can hear a herd's bony ankles "clicking" as they trot across the tundra, and caribou grunt to communicate as they move.

Caribou often travel at an effortless trot that really eats up ground. They can run up to 40 mph, which is faster than a whitetail deer. Also, caribou are excellent swimmers. Swift rivers and broad lakes do not slow them down. They just wade right in and go. It's not uncommon to see caribou swimming in the middle of large lakes, even out of sight of land.

Besides differences in physical characteristics, subspecies of caribou are designated by the region they inhabit. I will cover only the barren-ground subspecies here since those are the ones we saw and would be hunted by our NCOs.

Barren-ground caribou are large herd animals similar in size to mule deer. They migrate long distances and have calving grounds, generally above the tree line on the tundra in the summer. Then, they typically migrate further south in the winter to spend some time in more sheltered areas during the snow and cold seasons.

Eagle Village on the Yukon River

SOMEONE HAD BULLDOZED a landing strip along a ridgeline southwest of Eagle Village on the Yukon River. The ridge was about a thousand feet in height and ran generally east to west, with a drop-off at the east end. The landing strip had not been used in some time and had sparsely-scattered one to two-foot-high vegetation growing on it. Otherwise, it was sufficiently long and usable to land an Otter on and was the only place to land other than the strip at Eagle Village, which was about fifty miles away.

We loaded up five of our NCOs, flew them to the ridgeline landing strip, dropped them off, and agreed to return in five days to pick them up. On the fifth day, Larry and I flew back to the ridgeline strip, where the NCOs met us after we landed.

They informed us that they had killed six caribou, one for each of them and one for Larry and me to share, on the condition that we carry it to be loaded on the Otter. We were more than happy to comply, and with the feet tied together and a long tree limb slid between them to rest on our shoulders, we carried it to the plane. With all the caribou loaded and the NCOs on board, we took off and flew them back to Fort Wainwright.

I WILL NOTE HERE that military flying restrictions were somewhat lax back then. If a pilot wanted to go flying, they signed the aircraft out and went flying. This applied only to the U-1A Otters and O-1 Bird Dogs, not to the U-21A turboprop.

WHEN MY IN-LAWS came to visit the following year, I cooked some of the caribou steaks. They were a little tough. As my father-in-law put it, *"You cooked them wrong. You were supposed to nail them to a board, cook them, throw away the steaks, and eat the board."*

Larry and I later took the rest of our caribou to a meat processing facility in Anchorage and had it all made into smoked sausage. It was delicious.

In memory of a special friend, Larry Lee Smithee. Larry passed on my birthday, May 19, 2023. He was 82 years old. GBNF, my friend.

CHAPTER 22
FORT YUKON

Fort Yukon, the state's largest Athabascan village, sits on the banks of the Yukon River in Interior Alaska, 8 miles north of the Arctic Circle. It is home to about 560 people and is 145 miles northeast of Fairbanks. Access to the village is primarily by air. However, in summer, the Yukon River serves as a "highway" for riverboats transporting friends and family between the many villages scattered along its length.

Fort Yukon is one of the older non-Native settlements in Alaska, founded as a fur-trading outpost in 1847 by the Hudson Bay Company. To this day, many residents earn their livelihoods through fur trading.

Fort Yukon Air Force Station (AAC ID: F-14, LRR ID: A-01) is a general surveillance radar station located 1.6 miles east-southeast of Fort Yukon, Alaska. The ground control intercept (GCI) station was closed on 1 November 1983 and redesignated as a Long-Range Radar (LRR) site as part of the Alaska Radar System. Today, it remains active as part of the Alaska NORAD Region under the jurisdiction of the 611th Air and Space Operations Center, Elmendorf AFB, Alaska.

GARY R. WILSON

. . .

Fort Yukon Village with Fort Yukon Air Force Station circled in red.

As I stated in the last chapter, military flying restrictions were somewhat lax when I was stationed in Alaska. If a pilot wanted to go flying, they signed the aircraft out and went flying. On several occasions during the summer months, I would fly up to Fort Yukon and visit with the Air Force personnel stationed at the Fort Yukon Air Force Station.

Having called ahead, they would have someone meet me at the airport to drive me to the site. I would shoot pool, drink coffee, and generally hang out with them for a few hours, then fly back to Fort Wainwright.

During the winter of 1970/71, a medical team was making its way on foot from Circle to Fort Yukon, testing some equipment in Arctic conditions. Radio communications had been lost with them, and I was assigned to fly two team members to Fort Yukon with replacement radios. It was 35 degrees below zero when I took off from Fort Wainwright in one of our U-1A De Havilland Otters. (Even the airlines stop flying at 30 below.)

Fort Yukon Airport

Upon landing at Fort Yukon, I was met by one of the Air Force personnel from the Air Force Station, who told me I was to go back with him and call my operations officer at Fort Wainwright. So, I shut down and went back with him. It was 65 below zero at Fort Yukon.

After making the call, I was transported back to the airport. I had been given another assignment to conduct a "range sweep" of an area where some type of test equipment that had been sent up into the sky was expected to fall. By then, I had been on the ground at Fort Yukon for 45 minutes.

THE OTTER's three-bladed variable-pitch propeller is moved to high pitch on shutdown, controlled by oil pressure flowing through the center nose cone of the prop assembly.

On takeoff, the prop control is moved to the full forward, flat pitch position, producing the most thrust and offering the least resistance for the prop to move through the air. It is taking a smaller bite of air, allowing for faster rotation. Sitting on the ground at -65 degrees temperature had thickened the oil to the point that the props would not cycle out of high pitch, low rpm.

Between the altitudes of one and two thousand feet, a temperature inversion occurs, and the temperature becomes warmer. Taking off at full rpm with the props at high pitch could over-boost the engine, so I elected to take off at reduced power, trusting the temperature inversion to be warm enough to allow the props to cycle to flat pitch high rpm. It worked. I made the range sweep and continued back to Fort Wainwright. Ho-hum.

CHAPTER 23
MICKEY MOUSE

Upon arrival back at Ft. Wainwright, I reported my non-textbook take-off procedure to maintenance, asking them to check the engine for a possible engine overboost. I wanted to be sure that the engine was undamaged and safe to fly.

The following day, as I was walking down the upstairs hallway in the hangar, the Deputy Battalion Commander, a Lt. Colonel, approached me and began chewing me out. He had received a copy of my report to maintenance and told me that I had possibly damaged a very expensive piece of government equipment, and he was going to see that I paid for it!

It should be noted here that this man was someone I considered a friend. Our families had visited in each other's homes many times, sharing meals and good times. I had also been his adjutant during which time I was instrumental in our unit passing an IG inspection with flying colors.

I was so surprised and hurt that I reacted out of my PTSD instead of common sense. I replied, *"Fine! I'm tired of this Micky Mouse outfit anyway!"* In aviation terminology, "he came to a low hover." *"Mickey Mouse! Mickey Mouse!"* he shouted. I just turned around and walked away. He had an Article 15 investigation initiated against me, and I had to appear in "court."

The UCMJ Article 15: Non-Judicial Punishment (NJP) is a disciplinary process that allows commanders to address minor offenses committed by service members. This process is known by different names depending on the branch of the military. In the U.S. Army and U.S. Air Force, it is referred to as Article 15. The Marine Corps calls it Office Hours. The U.S. Navy and U.S. Coast Guard call it Captain's Mast. Regardless of the name, the purpose of NJP is to discipline service members for minor offenses such as being late for duty, petty theft, damaging government property, sleeping on watch, providing false information, and disobeying orders. — Military Law Center

A major from Battalion HQ conducted the hearing, calling three witnesses as well as hearing my testimony. After hearing all witnesses and reviewing all evidence, I was 100% exonerated.

CHAPTER 24
NOME

From July 1969 to April 1971, I flew into Nome on several occasions, both in the U-1A Otter and the U-21A twin turboprop. I'll share two of the events with you here. The other times were just stopovers for refueling or short turnarounds.

Nome's oldest inhabitants were Iñupiat natives. The area came to Western attention in 1898 when three Nordic Americans discovered gold on the ocean shores of Nome, prompting the Nome Gold Rush. Within a year, the city went from non-existent to having a population of 10,000. Gold mining continued to attract settlers into the early 1900s, but the city's population had fallen considerably by 1910.

Between 1905 and 1974, fires and violent storms destroyed most of Nome's Gold Rush-era buildings. In the winter of 1925, a diphtheria epidemic raged among Alaska Natives in the Nome area.

Fierce, territory-wide blizzard conditions prevented the delivery of a life-saving diphtheria antitoxin serum by airplane from Anchorage. A relay of dog sled teams was organized to deliver the serum.

Today, the Iditarod Dog Sled Race follows the same route they took and ends in Nome.

My best friend and copilot, CWO2 Larry Smithee

IN MARCH 1970, my copilot, CWO2 Larry Smithee, and I were assigned to fly four Navy admirals to visit several Army National Guard locations. I hadn't a clue what business Navy admirals had with the Army National Guard, but "Ours is not to wonder why," etc.

The admirals were waiting for us in front of the Eielson Air Force Base tower, approximately 25 miles southeast of Fairbanks. After the admirals boarded, I taxied to the runway directly in front of the control tower for takeoff.

The tower radioed and asked if I would like to taxi to the departure end of the runway. Eielson's runway is 14,507 feet long, with the control tower centered on the east side, so I still had over 7,000 feet of runway for takeoff, more than enough for the U-1A De Havilland Otter we were flying. Therefore, I advised them I would take off from where I was. I applied power and lifted off about 500 feet down the runway. The tower radioed, *"I guess you didn't need all of the runway after all."*

Me in Bethel, Alaska

OUR FIRST STOP WAS BETHEL, Alaska. While the Admirals were off visiting the National Guard unit, Larry and I had time to kill, so we played around with a snowmobile one of the control tower personnel loaned us.

Whoo Hoo!

BETHEL, located on the Kuskokwim River 40 miles from the Bering Sea, 281 air miles from Nome, and 400 air miles from Anchorage, is a commercial center and port for the Yukon-Kuskokwim Delta region. It provides food, fuel, medical care, and other services for 56 surrounding villages. Home to a population of about 6,400 residents, Bethel is the largest rural community in Alaska.

Note the two-star plaque indicating general-grade passengers.

After the admirals returned, we flew them to Nome, where we would stay overnight. Our arrival in Nome coincided with the annual Iditarod Dog Sled Race. Hmmm. So that's why "Admirals" wanted to visit "Army" National Guard units in Nome.

Iditarod History

IN 1925, The Great Race of Mercy gained notoriety for its critical role in delivering medicine via sled dog during the Nome diphtheria epidemic. Sled dogs were brought out of near retirement when all other transportation routes, including air and railway, failed to deliver the much-needed serum to Nome's sick and dying children.

Mushers and sled dogs endured temperatures circling -80 degrees F, with complete whiteout conditions and unstable ice crossings. Against all odds, and through the work of 20 mushers – two-thirds of them Indigenous Peoples – and 150 sled dogs, the Serum Run was successful in delivering antitoxins to treat the sick children of the 10,000-person town.

The race reconstructs the freight route to Nome and commemorates the role that sled dogs played in the settlement of Alaska. The mushers travel from checkpoint to checkpoint, much as the early freight mushers did. Some modern dog drivers move at a pace that would have seemed impossible to their old-time counterparts, making the trip to Nome in under ten days.

The name Iditarod comes from the Deg Xinag and Holikachuk languages of the Athabascan people of Interior Alaska, meaning *distant* or *distant place*. It's not only the name of a trail but also the name of a former town and a river in the same region.

The race spans the Alaska and Kuskokwim Mountain ranges and follows the Yukon River for 150 miles. Mushers endure crossing frozen waterways and pack ice in Norton Sound, often completing the race in as little as eight days.

Iditarod racer arriving in Nome

AS IT TURNED OUT, the week-long Iditarod Basketball Tournament, the largest basketball tournament in the world, was also being played that week, so we hung out that evening to watch a game. It was standing room only.

While we were watching the game, a very pretty, blond-haired young woman approached me and introduced herself, adding that she was from Russia. She must have been relatively young when she came from Russia, as she had no noticeable accent. As interesting as getting better acquainted with her might have been, I sadly had to inform her that I was married.

After the game, we slept on cots in one of the gymnasium rooms. The next morning, we rounded up our admirals and prepared for departure to Tin City Air Force Station. Tin City is a Long-Range Radar Site located 106 miles west-northwest of Nome. We made a short stop there; then it was back to Eielson Air Force Base, where we said goodbye to our admirals.

Tin City Air Force Station

IN THE WINTER of 1969/70, we were assigned to fly replacement parts for Hueys stationed at Nome. Below-freezing temperatures played havoc with the Hueys, especially their hydraulic seals.

U-21A Ute

Taking off from Fort Wainwright in Army 18084, a twin-engine turboprop, we climbed to our cruising altitude for the flight. The weather was deteriorating rapidly as we neared Nome.

After switching to the Nome approach frequency, I heard a Wein

Air Alaska 717 pilot receiving landing instructions. Before landing, he radioed for me to be aware of a strong right crosswind on final approach. We were landing just in front of a blizzard blowing in off the Bering Sea from the south with a 30-40 knot crosswind!

Nome Airport
The Bering Sea is just off the picture to the left. We landed on the runway from the upper left to the lower right (west to east).

When I turned final, I had to crab to the right to stay on course for landing on runway 9. Just before landing, I dropped the right wing, added some left rudder (a maneuver known as a "slip"), and lined up with the runway. This maneuver is an aerodynamic condition of uncoordinated flight that is used to maintain the runway centerline during a crosswind landing. It can also be used to lose altitude quickly without increasing airspeed or forward motion.

I touched down on the right main landing gear, then dropped to the left main landing gear and nose gear, and used reverse pitch to slow us down on the packed snow on the runway. After taxing to our assigned parking, we securely tied down the plane and found transportation to Nome, where we found lodging at the North Star Hotel.

Upon waking the next morning, we found that we were snowed in and would not be able to leave for several days—poor us. We had to play tourist and draw TDY pay for the next three days.

CHAPTER 25
SAINT LAWRENCE ISLAND

In the summer of 1970, we were assigned the mission of flying a "fact-finding" team to Saint Lawrence Island. Both the Fort Richardson U-21A and our U-21A were used for this mission. We flew into Nome for refueling, then to Savoonga on Saint Lawrence Island.

To stay below Russian radar, we flew at 1000 feet for the 126-mile trip across the Bering Sea. It's commonly acknowledged in aviation that a single-engine plane starts running rough when crossing any significant body of water. Any engine problem beyond gliding distance from land is a critical problem, even if you have more than one. But when flying a single, it's everything.

Although we were flying twin-engine turboprops, we were only flying at 1000 feet for 126 miles each way, which significantly increases the "pucker factor."

Savoonga, Saint Lawrence Island, Alaska

UPON LANDING AT SAVOONGA, we had the opportunity to "play tourist" for a few hours. I met one of the local Army National Guard members who became my tour guide. He was very knowledgeable and filled me in on the history of Saint Lawrence Island. I also bought a couple of seal skins and an *"oosik"* from him.

An oosik is the bone of a walrus penis. An average walrus oosik is approximately 19.5 inches long, measured straight from tip to tip, which is about the length of the one I purchased.

Prior to the 20th century, oosiks were not often used by Alaska Native peoples, as this dense bone is difficult to carve. Only a handful of archaeological examples of carved oosiks exist. It appears that they were occasionally used as clubs and for the manufacture of handles and harpoon assemblies.

Of the two seal skins, one was a spotted seal, and the other was a ring seal. I still have part of one seal skin, but the oosik deteriorated and is no longer with us.

St. Lawrence Island, the sixth-largest island in the U.S., lies in the northern part of the Bering Sea, 126 miles southwest of Nome and 120 miles south of Bering Strait. It is 90 miles long and 1792 square miles in size. Its western extremity is only 40 miles from the Siberian coast, which is clearly visible in good weather; its eastern end is approximately 100 miles from the Alaskan mainland. The present population consists of 496 Eskimos belonging to the Yuit (Siberian) group, most living at Gambell (Sevuokuk) at the island's northwest end and Savoonga, 40 miles to the east.

Vitus Bering discovered the island on Saint Lawrence Day, August 10, 1728 (Old Style (O.S.) calendar), and named it Saint Lawrence.

In 1979, the BLM gave the native population interim conveyance of the island. They were to receive the final title when the government finished its survey of the island in 2016, when the villages of Gambell and Savoonga were returned ownership of Saint Lawrence Island with a title.

CHAPTER 26
SEARCH & RESCUE

Summer 1970

In Alaska, flying is often the only means of getting from one place to another, exposing pilots to many hazards, including treacherous mountain passes and volatile weather. A clear flight can quickly turn into a nightmare of clouds, rain, and wind as pilots attempt to navigate tricky mountain passes, glaciers, and rivers bordered by mountains.

There's a lot involved that you won't find in the Lower 48. It isn't as simple as taking all the classes and getting your license. You have to know where you are, where you're going, and how you're going to get there.

Making matters more challenging is the fact that Alaska has relatively few weather stations that can provide crucial information about flying conditions.

Alaska is a very challenging place to fly. Its terrain consists mainly of mountain ranges that generate their own weather, mountain passes, dead-end valleys, and glaciers that create their own weather.

Bottom line? You'd better know Alaska, or you can find yourself in trouble.

Map of Search & Rescue Area

THE SEARCH and rescue mission we were assigned to help with involved a missing 172 Cessna with three on board that had been en route from Anchorage to Whitehorse, Canada. Navigating that route in a small plane isn't a straight shot since you can't fly high enough to clear the mountains, requiring the pilot to maneuver around all these obstacles by staying in the valleys and flying over low mountain passes.

My copilot, CWO2 Larry Smithee, our crew chief, and one of our NCOs and I were going to be based out of McCarthy Creek, Alaska. The U.S. National Park Service had facilities and a small airstrip at McCarthy Creek, which included a small, minimally furnished house. We had cots, sleeping bags, C-rations, and other necessities for an extended stay. There were about eight of us staying there, as we had two Otters and crews involved in the search and rescue.

U.S. National Park Service Facility and Airstrip

Our search area extended east to Whitehorse, Canada, and south along the coast to Yakutat on the Gulf of Alaska. We landed once at Whitehorse for refueling.

Whitehorse is the city and capital [since 1952] of Yukon, Canada. It is located on the Yukon (Lewes) River just below Miles Canyon and the former Whitehorse Rapids. Yukon is a territory in the extreme northwestern corner of Canada. It is also the smallest and least populous Canadian territory.

Whitehorse was founded during the Klondike Gold Rush (1897–98) as a staging and distribution center. It was the head of river navigation and became the northern terminus of the White Pass and Yukon Route [railway] from Skagway.

Whitehorse, Canada

• • •

MANY VALLEYS in mountainous areas have wide openings but dead ends. The 172 Cessna was flying under cloud coverage that extended partway down the mountains, obscuring its view of needed terrain features. It was later found that they had turned too early into a dead-end valley. An experienced Alaskan pilot would have recognized his error and turned around. When mountains and clouds are all you can see, it's time to "get the heck out of Dodge."

The crash site was found by a helicopter crew after the weather had cleared. There were no survivors.

CHAPTER 27
THE WOOD RIVER

My in-laws came to visit in early August 1970. Let me begin by acknowledging that I had the best in-laws a man could ask for. My father-in-law was a retired Army master sergeant from Oklahoma, and my mother-in-law was a war bride from Japan. I loved them both. I took two weeks of leave in anticipation of their stay with us.

I HAD ALREADY MADE plans to camp with a few friends on the Wood River for a few days, so I proceeded to prepare for that. One of my crew chiefs worked for Northwest Airlines before entering the army and was friends with some of their pilots. Two of the pilots were planning to fly a Cessna 180 up from the Lower 48, pick up my crew chief at Fairbanks, and fly to their camping site on the Wood River. My crew chief had asked my friend CWO2 Larry Smithee and me to join them for a few days.

The plan was for them to set up camp, then one of the pilots would fly back to Fairbanks and pick up Larry and me. We were waiting at the airport for him, but when he didn't show up after two hours, we felt that something had happened and decided to go look for them.

When I returned to my apartment to change into my flight gear, I asked my father-in-law if he wanted to go for a ride. I then drove to Fort Wainwright, where I met up with Larry and signed out an Otter. Four of us, including my father-in-law and our crew chief, were on board for our "search and rescue" flight.

The Wood River is a small river that runs north out of a valley in the Alaska Range of mountains. It eventually intersects with the Tanana River southwest of Fairbanks. North is at the bottom of the image.

UPON ARRIVAL in the area of the Wood River, where I knew the camp was to be set up, we saw what had happened. Instead of landing lengthwise on a long, wide gravel bar, they had tried landing across its widest point to avoid a tree root sticking up in the air near one end of the long axis of the bar. It would've worked except for a shallow wash they couldn't see from the air. They had made a good landing, but when they came to the wash, the plane tipped forward, damaging the prop.

After making a couple of low passes over the area, Larry suggested that we had enough room to land just beyond the root. Larry had much more flying time in the Otter than I did, having flown them in Vietnam, so I leaned more on his judgment. After we were on the ground, he would use our survival axe to cut the root off, giving us enough room for takeoff.

Otter with flaps lowered to about 40 degrees. Note that the aileron drops down also.

I set up a straight-in approach for landing. When I judged the height and angle to be correct, I lowered full flaps. The Otter has full-span slotted flaps, the outer portions acting as ailerons. The flaps are at 45 degrees when fully extended, requiring the yoke to be pushed forward against the stops to keep flying. It feels like you are flying straight toward the ground. At the right moment, when properly executed, the yoke is pulled back against your chest, all three of the landing gear touch down simultaneously, and the plane comes to a stop.

As I was on short final for landing, I noticed that the three men on the ground were watching us as if we were crazy, and one was taking pictures. I somehow did everything right. We barely cleared the root; I pulled the yoke to my chest and made a perfect three-point landing, stopping just short of the river.

After shutting down, we all exited the aircraft. The two crew chiefs and I pushed the plane's tail around opposite the way we had landed, then pushed it back as close to the river as we could get it while Larry chopped the root off. He then walked the gravel bar to ensure it was clear of any other obstacles. We loaded everyone up, along with the camping equipment of the three we were picking up, and prepared for takeoff.

I STARTED the engine and went through the preflight checks while Larry set the flaps to be lowered. The flaps on an Otter are lowered manually by pumping a hydraulic lever located on the floor between the pilot and copilot seats. A selector switch is flipped up to raise the flaps and flipped down to lower the flaps. Larry was ensuring that it was in the down position.

The procedure for a short-field takeoff in the Otter is to leave the flaps up until the tail comes off the ground, then rapidly lower the flaps. The Otter can gain speed more quickly with the flaps up. It is generally known that the Otter will fly once the tail starts flying.

Larry had a grip on the flap pump lever; the prop was set at flat pitch, high rpm, so I pushed the throttle fully forward, and we started rolling. When we had gained enough airspeed for the tail to come off the ground, I eased the yoke forward to level us out. Larry began to pump that lever like crazy, and we lifted off just as the river passed out of sight below the nose of the aircraft.

We were airborne and slowly gaining airspeed, so I gradually raised the flaps until they were fully up. We continued to gain altitude and airspeed and headed back to Fairbanks to drop off our three passengers and their camping equipment. Just another day of flying in "The Last Frontier."

> *"Even though I [fly] through the valley of the shadow of death,*
> *I will fear no evil,*
> *for You are with me."*
> **(Psalm 23:4a)**

CHAPTER 28
VALDEZ

O rca and humpback whales, otters, sea lions, and birds are among the many animals that live in Prince William Sound.

Pink and silver salmon are Pacific species that can be seen and caught in the waters of Port Valdez and Prince William Sound. The town of Valdez, Alaska, is one of the best pink and silver salmon fishing spots in Alaska.

Good salmon fishing can usually be had throughout the Arm and Narrows area by the end of July, and exceptional fishing in the Port by the first or second week of August. The fishing can then be great through Labor Day, with many fish in the 10 to 15-pound range and some at 20!

Early in the run, a boat is required to catch silvers and pinks. As the run comes in closer, salmon can be caught from shore at Allison Point and on the city side around the mouth of the small boat harbor.

My new bride and I planned several interesting trips and activities while my in-laws were with us. Their arrival in the first part of August 1970 coincided with the beginning of salmon fishing in Valdez, so one day, we drove down there to see if we could catch some.

My 1967 Austin Healy 3000 Mk 3 was only a two-seater and not very conducive to driving in Arctic conditions, so I purchased a used 1962 Willys Wagoneer to drive while we were in Alaska. It had plenty of room for everyone and our gear.

Worthington Glacier

We took the opportunity to play on a glacier near the highway on our way to Valdez. The Worthington Glacier is one of the most accessible glaciers in Alaska. It is located in Thompson Pass along the Richardson Highway and is impossible to miss if you are driving to or from Valdez. The glacier can be seen from the road while driving, or you can stop at the Worthington Glacier State Recreation Site to walk to the glacier. The glacier was closer to the highway the day we were there.

Upon arrival in Valdez, we rented a small aluminum boat like the one in the center of the above picture and set out to fish. In less than an hour, we caught ten nice salmon, each weighing over ten pounds.

The water was pretty crowded with small boats like ours; people were whooping and hollering, salmon were jumping out of the water all around us, and a couple actually jumped into nearby boats. There was almost a party atmosphere. It was the most fun day of fishing I had ever experienced.

My Japanese mother-in-law was the most excited of us all. You would think we had found gold instead of salmon. She cleaned the fish, cutting them open and saving the roe and eggs from each one as if they were gold nuggets.

When we got back to Fairbanks, she salted and wrapped two of the largest salmon, the roe, and the eggs in plastic, then newspaper, then more plastic, and more newspaper, then more plastic, in preparation for flying them back home with her. I think I made a lot of points with her that day.

CHAPTER 29
DALL SHEEP

Of all big game animals, I only ever wanted the trophy of a dall sheep head on my wall. No easily accessible "stands" or "feeders" are used to bag one of these majestic animals. If you want one of these trophies, you have to work for it. You won't find them on a hunting lease a short drive away or in any of the Lower 48 states.

Dall sheep inhabit some of Alaska's most rugged alpine areas. They thrive on the wind-swept, exposed cliffs and peaks of mountains in central and northern Alaska. This subspecies of sheep is found only in Alaska and western Canada. Dall sheep weigh an average of 130 pounds and have white fur. Rams have large horns that form a characteristic curl, while females, called ewes, have smaller horns.

Dall sheep are found in relatively dry country and frequent a combination of open alpine ridges, meadows, and steep slopes with extremely rugged "escape terrain" in the immediate vicinity. They use ridges, meadows, and steep slopes for feeding and resting.

Dall sheep are found in the Kenai Mountains, the Tok area, the

Chugach Mountains, Mentasta, Nutzotin, northern Wrangell Mountains, Tanana Hills, the White Mountains area, the Central and Eastern Brooks Range, and on the north side of the Alaska Range east of the Nenana River, west of the Delta River, and south of the Tanana River.

The area we were hunting is circled in red.

My friend Larry Smithee and I would be hunting this beautiful animal in the Alaska Range. We drove my 1962 Willys Wagoneer on the Parks Highway, which is paved and open all year, from Fairbanks to Healy. Just south of Healy, we turned east and followed a mostly dry stream bed for about 20 miles until it ended at the junction of two mountain ridges. It was there that we set up camp.

For the next three days, we hiked along mountainsides and ridges and across saddles and mountain passes, using inches-wide paths in slippery shale made by the dall sheep, looking for trophy rams. A ram's horn must have a three-quarter curl or more to be legal. For three days, we only saw ewes or very young rams. Sometimes, these came so close that we could almost touch them. They were leery but did not recognize us as a threat.

Finally, on the fourth day, as we were easing over a saddle, we saw six trophy-size rams in the valley below us. It took a couple of hours to stalk our trophies, carefully moving from cover to cover. Late in the afternoon, we eventually made our way, unseen, to a large boulder in the valley that would provide cover as we set up for a shot.

Larry was left-handed, so he was on the left side of the boulder, and I was on the right. We had confirmed which of the rams we would shoot and were taking aim when a hawk or eagle flew over and started screaming! The rams went up the other side of the valley like they were shot from a cannon! *Of all the blankety, blank, blank luck! Shoot! Crap! Dang! I need a big, tall glass of "iced tea!"* Well, I am a Baptist.

We made our way back to the campsite just before dark. It had been a wonderful four-day experience. We had a great time and enjoyed the beauty of God's creation, but we had to leave the next day, so our chance at a trophy dall sheep was gone. Larry returned later with another friend and got a grizzly but no dall sheep.

I DID a lot of hunting in Alaska, filling my freezer with snowshoe rabbits, ptarmigan, and grouse. But, there was no trophy dall sheep head for my wall. I had to settle for an ivory carving from Point Hope, Alaska, that I purchased while in Nome.

Among the first people to do fine work in walrus ivory were an unknown group who lived on the western coast of Alaska more than a thousand years ago, before the Eskimos came. Some years ago, Dr.

Froelich Rainey and Helge Larsen of the Danish National Museum found very intricate carvings from this so-called "Ipiutak culture" near Point Hope. The Alaskan Eskimos, living south of Point Hope and out on the islands of the Bering Sea, have carried on the ancient heritage of walrus ivory carving. Their carvings are considered the most intricate and detailed of Alaskan carvers and the most desired.

CHAPTER 30
MT. PAVLOF VOLCANO

On 26 August 1970, C-124 Globemaster 52-1049 of the Georgia Air National Guard's 165th Military Airlift Group took off from McChord Air Force Base, Washington, bound for Cold Bay, Alaska. The C-124 transport plane was carrying seven tons of satellite observation equipment for use with the Optical Satellite Observing System from Tacoma (TCM) to Cold Bay (CDB). Ninety miles from the destination, aircraft commander Maj. William Goggans of Savannah and co-pilot 2nd Lt. Bobby Bowen of Atlanta made radio contact with ground control.

C-124 Globemaster

· · ·

In limited visibility, the crew started the descent to Cold Bay when the four-engine aircraft struck the slope of Mt. Pavlof, located 36 miles northeast of Cold Bay. The aircraft disintegrated on impact, and all seven crew members were killed. It is believed that the crew started the descent prematurely.

When the aircraft missed its expected 10:00 p.m. landing time, the Alaska Air Command Rescue Coordination Center at Elmendorf Air Force Base near Anchorage initiated search and rescue operations. The search was immediately hampered by poor weather conditions and the vast 4,500-square-mile search area encompassing remote mountainous regions and the open ocean. Eight aircraft from California, Hawaii, and Japan contributed to the search effort, while two Coast Guard vessels initiated sweeps of the Pacific Ocean.

On Sunday, 30 August 1970, an Air Force C-130 discovered the wreckage of 52-1049 on the slope of 8,200-foot Mt. Pavlof northeast of Cold Bay. The Globemaster had struck the mountain at more than 200 miles per hour, scattering wreckage over a wide area 200 feet from the summit of the snow-swept peak.

Once the crash site was determined, the army mountain climbing team from Ft. Greely, Alaska, was dispatched to Mt. Pavlof to search for survivors. My copilot, CWO3 "Doc" Waters, and I were assigned to fly the Ft. Greely post commander to Cold Bay.

We took off from Wainwright Army Airfield en route to Ft. Greely in Army 18084, a Beech Queen Air that had been upgraded with King Air wings and turboprop engines, giving it the additional power needed for short-field takeoffs. After picking up the post commander, we continued on to Cold Bay, where we stayed overnight before returning to Ft. Wainwright.

The Air Force personnel traded medical and other needed

services to the locals for things like "bounty from the sea." The local fishermen had caught Alaskan King Crab before we arrived, and we were surprised with trays piled high with King Crab legs and bowls of melted butter. I was ready to apply for an inter-service transfer to the Air Force with an assignment to Cold Bay! I almost made myself sick eating King Crab. It was literally "all you can eat" King Crab night!

Cold Bay, Alaska

SEVERAL ATTEMPTS WERE MADE to reach the crash site by the team, but the remains of the crew were never recovered. The tragedy marked the first loss of life for the Georgia ANG, which has been flying air transport missions worldwide since it began flying in 1961.

CHAPTER 31
FORT GREELY

Home to the U.S. Army Launch site for anti-ballistic missiles and one of the coldest places in Alaska, Fort Greely was established in 1942 as an Army Air Corps Base. It was originally called Big Delta Army Air Base, then Allen Army Airfield. The base was used as a rest and refueling area for American planes flying supplies to Russia for their use on the Eastern Front.

Mt. Hayes in the Alaska Range and the Tanana River to the north of Fort Greely

During World War II, Alaska was a major United States Army Air Force (USAAF) location for personnel, aircraft, and airfields to support Lend-Lease aid for the Soviet Union. In addition, it was in Alaska that the Empire of Japan bombed and seized United States soil. As a result, the USAAF was actively engaged in combat operations against them.

After WWII, the site was deactivated briefly but later reactivated in 1948 as an Army post. It was initially renamed Big Delta Alaska but was redesignated as the Army Arctic Center in 1952. The Army Arctic Center consisted of the Army Arctic Indoctrination School, the Army Training Company, and the Test and Development Section. All three of these were established to train Armed Services personnel to live and move in extreme subarctic and arctic conditions and to test the cold tolerance of assorted equipment.

At the same time, the U.S. Army Chemical Corps Arctic Test Team was established at the post, and major construction for permanent buildings began. In 1955, the post was renamed Fort Greely after Arctic explorer Major General Adolphus Greely. In the early 1960s, Fort Greely was a nuclear reactor site, partially for testing in arctic conditions and partially for power generation in a remote area. This reactor was shut down and removed in a few years.

FORT GREELY IS AN "OPEN" post, and buffalo roamed freely throughout the post, including the runways. When attempting to land, I often had to buzz the runway to clear it of buffalo before landing.

Buffalo at Fort Greely

Due to its location near the Alaska Range, it is often susceptible to crazy winds and wind currents, which can make landing tricky or impossible. I frequently had to make several attempts, with the winds throwing the Otter around like the mechanical bull at Gillies, before finally being able to land. A couple of times, I could not land at all. Between the buffalo, the crazy winds, and the winter snow and icing conditions, Fort Greely presented many challenges when attempting to land.

CHAPTER 32
KOTZEBUE

Otto Von Kotzebue, a Russian sailor, discovered Kotzebue Sound in 1818 while searching for the Northwest Passage. Kotzebue is a gateway to northern Alaska's Kobuk Valley National Park and other natural attractions. Kotzebue is on the Baldwin Peninsula in Kotzebue Sound, 33 miles north of the Arctic Circle. Most residents (over 75 percent) are Inupiat, descended from the first people to cross the Bering Sea Land Bridge. The Inupiat have inhabited the site for at least 600 years.

Owing to its location and relative size, Kotzebue served as a trading and gathering center for the various communities in the region. The Noatak, Selawik, and Kobuk Rivers drain into the Kotzebue Sound near Kotzebue to form a center for transportation to points inland. In addition to people from interior villages, inhabitants of far-eastern Asia, now the Russian Far East, came to trade at Kotzebue. Furs, seal oil, hides, rifles, ammunition, and seal skins were some of the items traded. People also gathered for competitions like the current World Eskimo Indian Olympics. The trading center expanded with the arrival of the whalers, traders, gold seekers, and missionaries.

Kotzebue Airfield

Kotzebue is also known as *Qikiqtaġruk*, which means "small island" or "resembles an island" in the Iñupiaq language. In the words of the late Iñupiaq elder Blanche Qapuk Lincoln of Kotzebue: *"When we were children, there was water behind front street and a slough between the Ipalooks and Adams'. There was another slough over between Coppocks and Lena Norton's house...The island on Front Street led to Kotzebue being called Qikiqtaġruk because island in Iñupiaq is called qikiqtaq."*

Kotzebue

KOTZEBUE IS another of those Alaska memories with nothing more interesting to add other than I've been there.

CHAPTER 33
FLYING INTO MIDNIGHT

Winter - 1970/71

Snow was falling as Army 18084, a modified Beech Queen Air, taxied from the hangar in the mid-morning darkness of the Alaskan winter. The Army U-21A Ute (Queen Air) had been upgraded with King Air wings and turboprop engines, giving it the additional power needed for short-field takeoffs.

As we taxied to the tower side of Wainwright Army Airfield to pick up our VIP passengers, the taxi lights of the sleek twin-engine turboprop stabbed into the darkness as if trying to capture some of the softly falling snowflakes in its beams. In the dimly glowing cockpit lights, I glanced across at my co-pilot. He appeared nervous as he concentrated on the IFR charts for the flight from Fairbanks to Richardson Army Airfield near Anchorage. Earlier, he expressed concern for the reported icing conditions en route and the moderate to heavy snowfall at both airfields. He was new at flying in these conditions, so I tried to assure him that our aircraft and we could handle it.

We arrived at the parking apron, where our VIPs were waiting to board. They were from the United States Army Alaska Headquarters at Ft. Richardson near Anchorage. Our mission was to fly them back to Ft. Richardson.

After all passengers were on board with seatbelts securely fastened, we received clearance to taxi to the departure end of runway 25 for takeoff. Once in position, I made one more check of the instruments, then eased the throttles full forward. The thrust of the powerful twin turboprops pressed me back in my seat. Rapidly gaining speed through the heavily falling snow, Army 18084 smoothly lifted off and climbed steadily into the dark Arctic sky.

As with every IFR takeoff, I experienced a feeling unlike any other. From that moment until I landed at my destination, I relied entirely on my instruments and instructions from air traffic control. It's rather exhilarating.

U-21 Cockpit with no outside visibility

From the time we took off, we began experiencing icing conditions, with a layer of ice building up on the leading edges of our wings and props. Our aircraft was equipped with de-icing boots, heated props, and a heated windscreen, so this was not a problem. The ice automatically cleared from the heated props and windscreen, but the de-icing boots were manually activated. A switch on the instrument panel was flipped, and air pressure inflated the boots, causing the ice to break loose and depart.

The crew has to wait for enough ice to build up on the wings' leading edges before activating the boots. Otherwise, the boots will push the thin layer of ice out, creating a gap when the boots deflate. Further icing will build up on that layer, and the boots will no longer be effective because of the gap created by activating them too soon. Hopefully, you can find a place to land before you run out of airspeed and altitude at the same time.

There are lights on either side of the fuselage that can be turned on to illuminate the leading edges of the wings. My co-pilot kept turning the lights on and asking if we needed to activate the boots. I kept telling him we needed more ice to build up first. Finally, he reached over to activate the boots without asking. I was barely able to knock his hand away in time. If he had succeeded, we would have been in deep doo-doo.

Mt. McKinley before Obama changed it to Denali

I ALWAYS ENJOY FLYING this route as we fly over the mountains of the Alaska Range and pass Mt. McKinley en route. Neither would be visible today as darkness, clouds, and falling snow obscured them. As I leveled off at 13,000 feet, the crew and passengers settled in for the hour and fifteen-minute flight south to Ft. Richardson.

The flight was otherwise uneventful until we were handed over to approach control in Anchorage. I was paying close attention to my instruments and the instructions from approach control when my co-pilot asked, *"What's that noise?"*

Now, I'm very sensitive to every sound and vibration in the aircraft, and to get a question like that when I'm trying to concentrate on many things at once to get us safely on the ground is a little disconcerting. Thankfully, I quickly picked up the faint noise of our FM radio station and flipped the switch to turn it off. "Problem" solved. We made our approach and landed without further disruptions.

THE WEATHER HAD NOT IMPROVED, so I elected to make the return flight myself instead of switching with my copilot. Usually, one pilot will fly "first pilot" one way, and the other will fly the return leg, allowing both to log "first pilot" time. Since my copilot was inexperienced and more than a little nervous, I flew the return leg myself.

The reported weather at Fort Wainwright was heavy snowfall with limited visibility, which would necessitate an instrument approach for landing. Flying in AI (actual instrument) conditions, a pilot has no visibility beyond the cockpit; therefore, focusing on his instruments is a priority.

After crossing the Alaska Range, there was no air traffic control, so flying was from VOR/ADF to VOR/ADF (very high frequency (VHF) omnidirectional range/automatic direction finding) ground base stations. *Automatic direction finding (ADF) is an electronic aid to navigation that identifies the relative bearing of an aircraft from a radio beacon transmitting in the MF or LF bandwidth, such as a Non-Directional Beacon or commercial radio broadcast station.*

I began my descent for a VOR approach to landing at Fort Wainwright (Wainwright Army Airfield) on runway 25. A VOR Approach is a non-precision approach providing lateral guidance only. When I arrived at the VOR, I intersected the outbound leg for my instrument approach.

Just a reminder that there was "zero" outside visibility

THE IDEA behind many instrument approaches is to track a final approach course that's aligned with the destination runway, in other words, to make a straight-in approach. Sometimes, this means flying outbound on the final approach course, then turning around to intercept the straight-in, final approach segment, or, in other words, making a procedure turn.

When flying VFR, reversing course is usually no big deal. If you want to turn, you clear the area to look for any potential conflict with other aircraft or obstructions, then go ahead and make your move. In the instrument-flying world, things are more regimented, especially when it comes to instrument approaches. Turning an airplane is never more complicated than reversing course to fly a segment of an instrument approach, knowing there are obstacles nearby. The procedure turn is one of the most confusing aspects of instrument flying.

. . .

IF A PROCEDURE TURN is depicted on an instrument approach chart, and you have been cleared for the approach without being on a radar vector to intercept the final approach course, *you must fly the procedure turn*. A procedure turn is flown exactly like the chart depicts. Entering the outbound leg at the initial fix, the pilot flies outbound on the defined radial, initiating a turn inbound at the designated point or distance.

When a teardrop procedure turn is used, it must be flown precisely as charted. From the outbound heading, a 45-degree turn is made toward the protected side. The pilot then flies outbound on that heading for about a minute and makes a 180-degree turn back toward the inbound leg. Teardrop procedure turns are rare and mostly found at military or joint-use airports.

Procedure turns are designed to clear obstacles in an area defined by the maximum entry altitude and the procedure turn distance. Usually, any entry altitude is permitted, but restrictions can allow for a smaller protected area.

Within the maneuvering area is a straight segment aligned with the inbound heading extending from the completion fix to the procedure turn distance. This segment provides obstacle clearance below the procedure turn altitude. *It's important to note that the area where the straight segment guarantees obstacle protection is much smaller than the procedure turn maneuvering area.* That is why pilots must not descend below the procedure turn altitude until they are established on the inbound heading. Below is a depiction of a procedure turn, although not the one I was making.

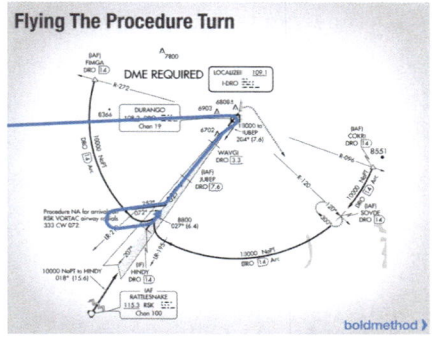

I was approaching from the south, and as I banked right to intercept the outbound leg of the instrument approach, I realized there was a crosswind from the south, requiring me to "crab" into the wind to stay on course. Since my procedure turn was to the right, flying into a headwind, I flew a longer outbound leg on the procedure turn to allow for the tailwind on the inbound leg. I did not want to overshoot the inbound final approach heading.

The importance of all these details becomes more apparent when you know there is a range of low-lying mountains not far to the north of the approach for landing on runway 25.

When we made the left turn onto the inbound leg or final approach to runway 25, we were in a total whiteout condition. My copilot radioed the tower to turn on the approach strobe lights to help orient us to the runway. The lights were barely visible under the snow.

Although the runway had been recently "plowed" clear of snow, there was still a hard-packed layer on the runway, and the runway lights were not visible due to the heavy layer of snow on either side. To show the parameters of the runway, 5-6-foot-tall "Christmas trees" had been stuck in the snow along the sides. I was below minimum altitude when I had the trees in sight and landed safely.

GARY R. WILSON

*"And I will lead the blind in a way that they do not know,
in paths that they have not known I will guide them.
I will turn the darkness before them into light,
the rough places into level ground.
These are the things I do, and I do not forsake them."*
(Isaiah 42:16)

CHAPTER 34
BARROW

L ocated on the Arctic Ocean, Utqiaġvik (formerly known as Barrow) is one of the largest Iñupiaq settlements in Alaska and the northernmost community in the United States. Its extreme location means Utqiaġvik receives 24-hour daylight from May 10 to August 2 and 24-hour darkness from November 18 to January 23.

Formerly known as Barrow, the village's official name was changed to Utqiaġvik in 2016 when village residents voted to return it to its traditional Iñupiaq name. Utqiaġvik is not accessible by road; the only way to get there is by plane.

Utqiaġvik is one of the oldest inhabited town sites in the United States, and archaeological evidence of human habitation in the area goes back to 800 AD. In the Inupiaq language, Utqiaġvik means "the place where we hunt snowy owls," but that's just one of the species that have lived here and provided food for local people for thousands of years.

Hunting and gathering are still a big part of life in Arctic Alaska, and seasonal hunts for whales, seals, walrus, caribou, and ducks remain essential for traditional and economic reasons. Today, Utqiaġvik serves as a hub community for smaller outlying villages, and its population of about 4,300 residents makes it one of Alaska's larger villages.

Whale Bone Arch

SEVERAL NEARBY SITES are on the National Register of Historic Places: the Cape Smythe Whaling and Trading Station, the Will Rogers and Wiley Post Monument, and the Birnirk Archaeological Site. The Cape Smythe Whaling and Trading Station, built in 1893, is the oldest frame building in the Arctic. The Whale Bone Arch beside the building is located right on the edge of the Arctic Ocean.

The Will Rogers and Wiley Post Monument, which was dedicated in 1982, is located across from the airport. The monument honors pioneer Wiley Post and comedian and homespun philosopher Will Rogers, who died in 1935 when their plane went down 15 miles southwest of Utqiaġvik during a flight to Siberia.

Approximately two miles north of the Utqiaġvik airfield is the Birnirk Archaeological Site. The Birnirk culture, which existed about 500 - 900 AD, is represented by 16 dwelling mounds and is considered a critical link between the prehistoric cultures of Alaska and Canada. The mounds reach up to 14 feet tall, with dwellings framed by driftwood and whalebones. Tools and other artifacts recovered from the site are used to compare artifacts from different sites and learn more about the Iñupiat culture in Alaska and Canada. Similar tools and artifacts have been found in the Russian Far East and northern Canada.

Airport

My company commander and I departed Fort Wainwright in Army 18084 in January 1971 for Barrow, Alaska. We were delivering hydraulic seals for the Hueys assigned there. The extreme cold made their hydraulic seals brittle, causing them to fail. Our crew chief accompanied us on this flight and kept the onboard coffee maker doing its thing.

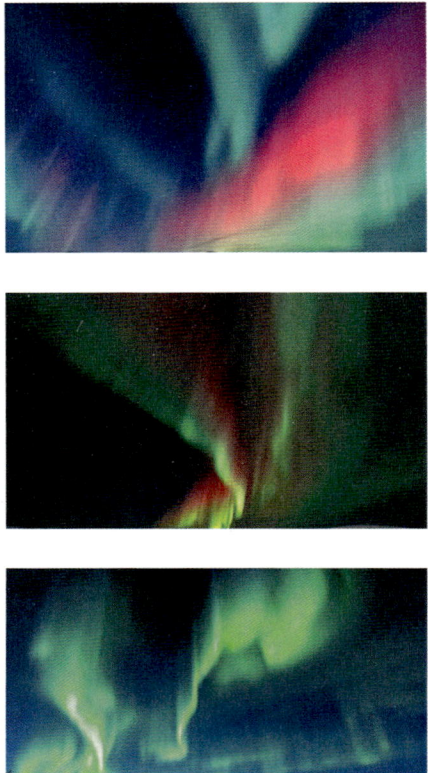

WE WERE TREATED to beautiful aurora borealis displays en route to Barrow and on our return flight. It was an uneventful flight with a quick turnaround at Barrow. My company commander and I switched seats while on the ground, allowing me to fly back and log "first pilot" time. Other than my crew chief accidentally dropping a cup of hot coffee in my lap shortly after takeoff, the return flight was also uneventful.

CHAPTER 35
LEAVING ALASKA

When the time neared for transfer to my next duty assignment, I called my branch officer to discuss my options. I wanted to fly the OV-1 Mohawk, but he said that since I was already multi-engine qualified, that would not be an option. That didn't make any sense to me, but the Army wasn't always noted for making good sense. He said I could either go to jump school or Huey transition. As any aviator will tell you, they will not jump out of a perfectly good airplane, so I chose the Huey transition option.

I ARRIVED a few days early at Fort Rucker, Alabama, in April 1971 with a pregnant wife due to give birth in May. After we settled into our mobile home rental, I reported to the Aviation School. Since I had some time to kill (Did I mention that my wife was due to give birth to our first child soon?), I decided to check out a U-6A De Havilland Beaver and fly around south Alabama in it for the next few days.

U-6A Beaver

Then began a new and exciting adventure for me. I was going to learn how to fly helicopters. I never had any desire to fly helicopters, but once we got started, I loved it. The initial training was in the OH-58A Kiowa, the Army version of the Bell Jet Ranger. The final phase of the transition course was in the UH-1B, D, & H model Hueys. What an incredible experience! Of all the aircraft I have flown, I loved the Huey best.

OH-58A Kiowa

A FIXED-WING aircraft is flown from the left seat, but a helicopter is flown from the right seat. When you settle into the Huey's cockpit, it feels like you are wrapped in a warm embrace. It's like a love affair to feel the thumping of the rotors lift you gently up in the air, float you smoothly over one spot, or take you anywhere you want to go. The two become one. The sound of a Huey is like no other and will forever be etched in my memory.

UH-1 Huey

When flying a fixed-wing aircraft, you taxi to the runway, line up with it, apply power, and take off. When flying a helicopter, it becomes an extension of the pilot, moving at a slow hover, forward and back, side to side, or moving into translational lift and flying. It basically does whatever you want it to do.

It has been said that a helicopter doesn't fly; it beats the air into submission. But I agree with Igor Sikorsky. *"The helicopter approaches closer than any other [vehicle] to fulfillment of mankind's ancient dream of the flying horse and the magic carpet."*

UH-1H Huey Cockpit

A HELICOPTER'S ability to move laterally in any direction or rotate 360 degrees makes it exciting to fly, but piloting one of these machines requires excellent skill, dexterity, and coordination. To control a helicopter, the pilot holds the cyclic, which controls all lateral movement with his right hand, and the collective, which controls lift with the left hand. At the same time, his feet must operate the foot pedals that control the tail rotor, which allows the helicopter to rotate in either direction on its horizontal axis and provides coordination in a turn. It takes both hands and both feet to fly a helicopter!

Hueys and Heroes

Upon completing the transition course, I received orders for a second Vietnam tour. I spent my leave time in Seaside, California, at the home of my in-laws, where my wife and newborn daughter would be staying while I was in Vietnam.

To reward myself for learning to fly helicopters and "because I was going back to Vietnam," I bought myself the car of my dreams—a 1971 911 Porsche!

1971 911 Porsche

Then, I received a surprise call from my branch officer informing me that my orders to Vietnam had been canceled! I was to report to Personnel, Fort Ord, for assignment as Company Commander of a basic training unit. Nine months later, I received my separation papers. The Army was kicking me out!

Although I only had a high school education, it was enough for me to hold the rank of Captain, fly multiple models of fixed-wing and rotary-wing aircraft, and lead men into combat when they needed "cannon fodder" in Vietnam, but it wasn't enough during peacetime. I have not piloted an aircraft since.

A$_{\text{FTER}}$ SEPARATING FROM THE ARMY, I went into law enforcement. I became a police officer with Seaside PD in Seaside, California. I had wanted to apply to become a commercial airline pilot, but my wife was back home and did not want to leave again. Anyhoo...that's another story.

GARY R. WILSON

"For You are my hiding place; You protect me from trouble. You surround me with songs of victory.
The LORD says, 'I will guide you along the best pathway for your life. I will advise you and watch over you.'"
(Psalm 32:7-8)

Afterword
SOMETIMES LIFE IS LIKE LOSING AN ENGINE ON TAKEOFF.

My daddy died of cancer when I was ten years old. Everyone I knew, including me, was praying that God would heal my daddy, but He didn't. Instead, He let my daddy suffer with terrible pain for two years before he died. He was only 45 years old.

A.D. Wilson

AFTERWORD

Jesus said, "A new commandment I give to you, that you love one another: just as I have loved you, you also are to love one another." **(John 13:34)**

My daddy *lived* that "new" command, yet God let him suffer and die anyway! I was very angry with God, and that anger continued well into my adult life! For many years, I questioned why God would let a good person, like my daddy, die so young — someone who loved Him and lived his life loving others. Someone who had a wife and two young children who needed him.

Me with my daddy - A. D. Wilson

Looking back over my life, I still don't understand it. But I see this: I would probably still be living on a farm in West Texas (not necessarily a bad thing). My two beautiful children, Lenore and Kevin, would not exist, nor would any of my life as I know it now, and all it entails exist. Romans 8:28 says, *"And we know that for those who love*

God all things work together for good, for those who are called according to His purpose."

Sounds good, but how does it keep us from hurting when things go wrong? No, it doesn't. But with God, life has a purpose beyond ourselves. And if you think life has thrown you more than your share of curveballs, consider what it would have been like if God hadn't been there running interference (I know; two different sports analogies).

We all have *"pivotal circumstances"* in our lives. Unexpected life events can be significant factors in how we perceive God. One of the wealthiest men in America, who has impacted every one of our lives through his development of international media distribution, grew up wanting to be a missionary. When he was young, his sister contracted leukemia. He and his family were told she would survive if they prayed and had enough faith. When she didn't, he decided that if there was a God, He certainly could not be trusted. He walked away from faith and never looked back.

When he was 13, Steve Jobs had a similar crisis of faith. He saw a picture of two children on the front cover of *Life* magazine, taken in a war-torn region of Biafra. He could not reconcile that picture with what he was being taught in the Lutheran church he attended. He asked the church's pastor if God knew what was happening in Biafra. The answer he received was less than acceptable. Steve Jobs never went back to church.

In both of the above cases, it wasn't the events that undermined their faith; it was their *interpretation* of the events as they related to God. These two men, and many other men and women throughout history, accomplished great things *without God*. But nothing we accomplish is truly done without God. We just lose the blessing of knowing that God was doing it "through us." As we pat ourselves on the back, thinking we did it, God sadly shakes His head.

"Do not lay up for yourselves treasures on earth, where moth and rust destroy and where thieves break in and steal, but lay up for yourselves

treasures in heaven, where neither moth nor rust destroys and where thieves do not break in and steal. For where your treasure is, there your heart will be also." **(Matthew 6:19-21)**

Anything we do or accomplish for ourselves will die with us. But people still remember my daddy, whose memory has been passed down to their children, as I am doing with my children now, because of how he lived his life for God and others. Micah 6:8 says, *"He has told you, O man, what is good; and what does the Lord require of you but to do justice, and to love kindness, and to walk humbly with your God?"*

I have learned and do know this: life isn't about us. Even though we have been taught from birth that it is, life still isn't about us. When Joseph's brothers (who had sold him into slavery) stood before him, now the second highest ruler in Egypt, because of a 7-year famine, they were expecting Joseph to punish them. Instead, Joseph said, *"And now do not be distressed or angry with yourselves because you sold me here, for God sent me before you to preserve life"* (Genesis 45:5), and *"As for you, you meant evil against me, but God meant it for good, to bring it about that many people should be kept alive, as they are today…"* (Genesis 50:20). Our faith can either grow stronger or weaker during traumatic events. It depends on how we *interpret* those events as they relate to God.

Many verses tell us we cannot know the mind of God. He's either God or He isn't. Who am I to say He isn't the God the Bible says He is? And if He is that God, who am I to disobey Him? How do we know about God and who He is? The same way that we know about math, science, history, or any other subject of higher learning, we go to class (church), listen to the teachers/preachers, and study the Textbook (the Bible). Just like places of higher learning, not all churches are equal, and not all teachers/preachers are equal. You may have to shop around.

"Real" history and science both confirm the authenticity of the Bible *and its presentation of God, people, and events*. I consider this: If I am wrong about what I believe, when I die, I will not have lost anything. If, however, those who do not believe what the Bible says are wrong, when they die, they will have lost everything!

It was a very difficult time for my mother after my daddy died, but she never lost her faith in God. She went for counseling for a while and eventually was told to write about what she had experienced and was feeling, which she did. I still have what she wrote.

People who knew my daddy said he was the kindest and gentlest man they had ever met. I had been told that he wanted to be a doctor and had worked and saved up his money to pay for college. He was 32 when he and my mother got married. So, why would God let my daddy die? 1 Corinthians 13:11-12 says, *"When I was a child, I spoke like a child, I thought like a child, I reasoned like a child. When I became a man, I gave up childish ways. For now we see in a mirror dimly, but then face to face. Now I know in part; then I shall know fully, even as I have been fully known."* We can't see the future, but God can, and, more importantly, it's in His hands.

My daddy had two younger sisters, the oldest of whom was my Aunt Opal. Aunt Opal wanted to be a schoolteacher, but it wasn't considered necessary for girls to get a higher education back then, so my grandpa wouldn't pay for her to attend college. My daddy used money he had saved to pay for his sister's first two years of college, and my grandpa paid for the last two years.

A nephew, the oldest son of my daddy's oldest brother, wanted to go to college, but his daddy couldn't afford to pay his tuition, so my daddy paid it. The nephew, my cousin Clyde Lee Wilson, Jr., once told me, *"Gary, I don't mean to be sacrilegious, but other than Jesus Christ, your daddy was the best man who ever lived. He always put others before himself."*

Regrettably (one of many regrets), I didn't inherit those genes from my daddy, but... no one inherits them. That kind of love comes only through trust and faith in God, and a love for God that I didn't have for many years. Because of that, I became the first of too many people to let my kids down and betray their trust. I should have been a daddy who put them before himself, but I didn't. They once believed that God would "fix" things in their lives, but He didn't. So, why believe in a God like that?

God didn't promise that there would be no pain and suffering, just the opposite, but He has also promised to always be with us.

"Have I not commanded you? Be strong and courageous. Do not be frightened, and do not be dismayed, for the Lord your God is with you wherever you go." **(Joshua 1:9)**

"The Lord is near to all who call on Him, to all who call on Him in truth. He fulfills the desire of those who fear Him; He also hears their cry and saves them." **(Psalm 145:18-19)**

"Go therefore and make disciples of all nations, baptizing them in the name of the Father and of the Son and of the Holy Spirit, teaching them to observe all that I have commanded you. And behold, I am with you always, to the end of the age." **(Matthew 28:19-20)**

"For I am sure that neither death nor life, nor angels nor rulers, nor things present nor things to come, nor powers, nor height nor depth, nor anything else in all creation, will be able to separate us from the love of God in Christ Jesus our Lord." **(Romans 8:38-39)**

As parents, in our imperfect way, we will always be there to support our children, whether physically with them or not, but the Holy Spirit is always with us if we are God's children. We become His children when we put our faith and belief in Jesus, His son. If we don't, we are like a vapor that passes through, then is gone. Nothing we can accomplish in this life will be worth anything when we get to heaven, and God asks, *"Why should I let you in?"*

I am immensely proud of all my children and their accomplishments. As someone who, *finally*, loves God and believes what He says, I know that it is only because of Him that you have achieved that which makes me so proud of you.

AFTERWORD

We are not here by chance. God had it planned all along since before any of us existed! Throughout the Bible, there are scripture verses that tell us how God knew us before we were ever conceived:

"For we are God's masterpiece. He has created us anew in Christ Jesus, so we can do the good things <u>He planned for us long ago</u>." **(Ephesians 2:10) NLT**

"I will praise you because I have been remarkably and wondrously made! Your works are wondrous, and I know this very well." **(Psalm 139:14) CSB**

"It is not that we are competent in ourselves to claim anything as coming from ourselves, but our adequacy is from God." **(2 Corinthians 3:5) CSB**

"Before I formed you in the womb I knew you, and before you were born I consecrated you; I appointed you a prophet to the nations." **(Jeremiah 1:5)**

"Your eyes saw my unformed substance; in your book were written, every one of them, the days that were formed for me, when as yet there was none of them." **(Psalm 139:16)**

"Even as He chose us in Him before the foundation of the world, that we should be holy and blameless before Him." **(Ephesians 1:4)**

"The Lord called me from the womb, from the body of my mother He named my name." **(Isaiah 49:1b)**

I look at the many ways God has protected and blessed me. I *know* of at least five situations where I would have died or been severely injured except for God's protection. One was during a trip from California to Texas. When traveling through Indio, California, driving a U-Haul truck and towing a Volkswagen Rabbit, the traffic suddenly stopped in front of me. I applied my brakes but immediately realized I would not be able to stop without causing a 5-6 car accident. I turned the steering wheel to the right and drove into this wide, level ditch, which was devoid of obstructions, gave it the gas, passed everyone up, and was back on the highway.

Another was when I was on my way to visit my son in Mississippi, who was there for training. I was in a rental car between Vicksburg and Bovina, Mississippi. It was raining, and the clouds were so heavy that it was almost dark. I was in the left lane behind a semi with what appeared to be a large SUV behind me. All I could see of the semi was its taillights, and I kept glancing in the mirror at the SUV behind me. Suddenly, the semi's brake lights came on, and it was slowing fast. As I applied my brakes, I realized the SUV was not slowing, so I turned my steering wheel to the left and headed for the center divider.

Interstate 20 had a wide center divider in this area, but several small streams also crossed it. God allowed all of this to happen in an area free of obstacles. Just as I cleared the interstate, I heard a loud bang as the SUV collided with the rear of the semi. I gave it the gas, and just as I pulled even with the semi's cab, a mid-sized sedan came spinning across in front of me. It passed with sufficient space for me to drive between it and the semi, and shortly after, I was back on the interstate.

There were times in Vietnam, Alaska, and others when I do not doubt that God had His hand of protection on me. If you think about it, you can also recall times when God protected you.

I believe there is one true God, that He is the God of the Bible, and that the Bible is His inspired Word. I also know and believe that everything in the Bible is true. Although not everything in the Bible was written "to us," I believe everything was written "for us" and is *relevant* to our belief in Jesus and how we live our lives.

I also know that no one has ever been able or will ever be able to explain or defend everything in the Bible, and that the Bible is often taken out of context. And...... I believe that the Bible exists only because of Jesus' resurrection. Without Jesus' death and resurrection, there would be no need for the "Bible."

Finally (aren't you glad there is a "finally"?), we are what we think about. Colossians 3:2 says, *"Set your minds on things that are above, not*

AFTERWORD

on things that are on earth." So, like my daddy, I'm trying to follow Jesus' last command, *"A new commandment I give to you, that you love one another: **just as I have loved you**, you also are to love one another"* (John 13:34). The key here is Jesus' command, ***"Just as I have loved you."*** Think about that!

I haven't even come close to the kind of man my daddy was, but I'm working on it. I can say, like Paul, *"Not that I have already obtained this or am already perfect, but I press on to make it my own, because Christ Jesus has made me His own. Brothers, I do not consider that I have made it my own. But one thing I do: forgetting what lies behind and straining forward to what lies ahead, I press on toward the goal for the prize of the upward call of God in Christ"* (Philippians 3:12-14).

ABOUT THE AUTHOR

Gary R. Wilson is the author of a humorous and interesting cookbook of mouthwatering recipes and non-fiction Christian books. This is Gary's thirteenth book.

Westbrook, Texas, is a dry, hot place in the summer, cold in the winter, and windy much of the time. In 1945, it had a population of 600 people and eight businesses. Today, its population hovers around 200. The businesses, of which I am aware, are a post office "downtown" and a café at the east edge of town.

I sometimes tell people I was "born and raised" in the Southern Baptist Church. I still have the perfect attendance pens for the first nine years of my life, and until I left home after high school, church was a major part of my life. I had a "drug" problem back then. Every time the doors were open, I got "drug" to church!

The first nine years of my life were on a small farm southwest of Westbrook. Go south from I-20 on Hwy. 670, hang a right just past the cemetery on County Rd. 244, go almost to the end (about half a mile), and the house was on the left. I haven't been there in years, but I don't think the house is there anymore.

We had no indoor plumbing and, therefore, no indoor toilet, but our outdoor toilet was a "two-holer." We also had no electricity and used an "ice box" for things that needed to be kept cool. A block of ice, about 12 inches square, had to be put into the top of the ice box for cooling. I remember when my daddy, A.D. Wilson, took the wood stove out, which stood in a corner of the kitchen, because we had gotten butane for heating and cooking. Our cook stove burned kerosene until that time. This all occurred when I was still preschool age. Even after we got butane and electricity, we only had indoor plumbing to one faucet in the kitchen, so the outdoor toilet remained in use until we left. We had no TV or telephone.

In West Texas, every boy wants to be a cowboy. I was no exception. Don and Roy, two of my playmates, were cousins who were two years older than me. We would play "Cowboys and Indians" most of the time. Since they were so much "older," they would often exclude me from things or just ignore me when I came with them, anyway. I had a bad temper in those days, and they would deliberately do things to set it off!

When I did play "Cowboys and Indians" with them or some of my friends, I often wanted to be an Indian. I liked trying to keep them from seeing me. I always wanted to be part Indian, but genealogy research later in life showed that I was pure blood honkie, albeit a Heinz 57 one.

We had a couple of milk cows and some chickens, so part of our income was selling milk, butter, eggs, and sometimes vegetables in Colorado City, about 11 miles east of us. Our transportation was a wagon pulled by a team of two horses, Pat and Patches.

We only went to the "black" side of town. I can still see my daddy laughing and visiting with those ladies. It was obvious that my daddy loved and respected them, and they also loved my daddy. Our family was often invited to attend their church, and sometimes we did. I am grateful to have had two godly parents who raised me without racial prejudices.

I lived the first 13 years of my life in West Texas, after which I moved to Mississippi, then Louisiana (which I hated), where I finished the last four years of school. I graduated from high school in 1964 (the happiest day of my life)! After working in the oilfield for about six months, I began my college experience at Hardin-Simmons University in Abilene, Texas, in January 1965. Not finding college compatible with my restless spirit (and I hated school!), I joined the army on October 25th, 1965.

I eventually earned a commission as an infantry officer through Officer Candidate School. While in OCS, I applied for and was accepted to flight school and earned my wings in May 1968, upon which I received orders for the tropical paradise of South Vietnam.

From June 1968 to June 1969, I flew 1309 combat hours in the O-1 Bird Dog, 324 of them at night. I earned the Distinguished Flying Cross, Air Medal with 25 oak leaf clusters, Bronze Star, Vietnamese Cross of Gallantry, and numerous lesser medals.

I love riding motorcycles and owned several Hondas in the 1970s (a couple of 175s, a 550/4, and two 750/4s). From May 2009 until now (2024), I have owned five different Harley-Davidson motorcycles, the last of which is a 2019 CVO Road Glide (with modifications).

Other books by Gary R. Wilson:
MEMORIES: RECIPES FROM CALLOWAY CORNERS, LOUISIANA
PERSPECTIVE: THE BIBLE and other INCONVENIENT TRUTHS
THERE'S SOMETHING ABOUT A WOMAN: GOD'S GIFT TO MANKIND
WHERE THE EYES LEAD: A BIKER'S CODE TO UNLOCKING THE BIBLE
IT'S ALL ABOUT JESUS: APOLOGETICS MADE SIMPLE
LEST ANY SHOULD BOAST: IT'S A GIFT, NOT A PROFESSION
A BOX OF CHOCOLATES: HUMBLE IS AS HUMBLE DOES
HAVE YOU NOT READ?: REVELATION 1:1-3
ROMANS: A CRITICAL EXPOSÉ
EPHESIANS: A CRITICAL EXPOSÉ
ECSTASY LOST: ONE FLESH FOREVER?
A TIGER TALE or A TALE ABOUT A TIGER'S TAIL
EXPRESSIONS OF MYSELF: POEMS, SHORT STORIES & OTHER RAMBLINGS

All are available on Amazon.

Made in the USA
Coppell, TX
31 December 2025